"Here, take this," Mel said, passing her the umbrella.

"It's not raining anymore," Georgia said, passing it back. She warmed at the sweet gesture.

"You never know when you'll run into trouble. You can bring it back to the clinic tomorrow."

Who was this new Mel? Georgia accepted the umbrella. "Okay. Thanks."

"And listen. What you said." Mel paused and crossed her arms, leaning up against the wall. "I wouldn't consider that 'wrong.' You had an emotional response during a really hard time in your life. Maybe cut yourself a bit of slack."

Mel's words melted all over her like a soothing balm. "I appreciate that. It might be a little easier to do without a million people commenting on what a loose cannon I am."

"People can say all kinds of things hiding behind their computers. They don't count." If only that were true.

"They count when your job is hanging in the balance," Georgia said, but knowing it didn't count to Mel seemed like the only thing that really mattered in that moment. "But thanks."

"And hey. If your bosses need a reference, tell them to give me a call."

Dear Reader,

Welcome to the sparkling lakes of Sunset County, a fictional small town in Canadian cottage country, and a place I loved escaping to in my mind while writing this story at a desk in my basement during a long, cold pandemic winter.

For Georgia and Mel, it all starts with a kitten. Six kittens, actually, and one mother cat, but there's one little fur ball in particular who I consider to be their clever matchmaker.

When public relations agent Georgia arrives in Sunset County to escape a very public PR disaster of her own making and to settle her aunt Nina's estate, she finds the stray cats and delivers them to the arms of local veterinarian Mel Carter, who is much more open to taking in the animals than she is to any possibility of getting close to another woman.

With a cast of furry (and scaly) animal friends and the warmth of a small town that's as cozy as Aunt Nina's old corduroy couch, this romance is about the inevitability of mistakes, the healing power of forgiveness and the gift of opening up to the possibility of true love.

I hope you enjoy this book and find yourself rooting for Georgia and Mel the way I did while writing their story. I'd love to hear from you on Instagram—find me @elledouglaswriter.

Elle

The Vet's Shelter Surprise

ELLE DOUGLAS

HARLEQUIN
SPECIAL
EDITION

HARLEQUIN®
SPECIAL EDITION™

Recycling programs
for this product may
not exist in your area.

ISBN-13: 978-1-335-59436-5

The Vet's Shelter Surprise

Harlequin Enterprises ULC
22 Adelaide St. West, 41st Floor
Toronto, Ontario M5H 4E3, Canada
www.Harlequin.com

Printed in U.S.A.

Elle Douglas is a lover of '90s alternative music, a wannabe chef specializing in comfort food and a sometimes reluctant but usually dedicated gym-goer who lives in Toronto with her romance-muse wife and their cat, Lucy (or Lucifer, depending on the day). Between writing romance novels and working as a high school guidance counselor, Elle works exclusively in helping others find their happily-ever-afters. Visit her at elledouglas.com.

Books by Elle Douglas

Harlequin Special Edition

The Vet's Shelter Surprise

Visit the Author Profile page at Harlequin.com.

This book is dedicated to my strong,
dynamic and fun-loving aunts.
Thanks for always making me feel special and loved.

And to my nieces and nephews
(aka the Sleepover Squad): I promise to always
indulge your whims. (Even ice cream for breakfast.
Just don't tell your parents.)

Chapter One

"Now, you keep those claws away from my sleeve. This is cashmere," Georgia murmured to the first adorable, yet inconvenient ball of fluff that she gently separated from the rest of the kittens, all cuddled up beside their plump mother cat. She deposited it in the banker's box lined with dish towels as the little creature mewed and glared at her, then went in for the second, her hands protected by red oven mitts.

"Okay, okay, you'll all get your turn. I'm trying to help you here. Something tells me your fur likes water almost as much as my shoes do," she said, eyeing the soft brown suede of her brand-new ankle boots and shifting the umbrella wedged between her neck and shoulder. One by one, she moved the six kittens, the mother helping her by leaping into the box unassisted, nuzzling her babies and licking their foreheads as they jostled to be next to her.

Despite the rain, Georgia paused for a moment, taking in the sight of the mother cat's fierce love and protection, and her kittens' desperate battle for her affection and attention. While Georgia was no animal person, it was hard to deny how cute the little fluff balls were. They were adorable, but it would only get them so far. They'd soon realize they'd have to claw their own way forward in this world.

Only an hour ago, Georgia had discovered the cat and her kittens while taking the garbage out to the bins housed in the shed behind her aunt's lakefront cottage. Their gentle cries guided her to the dugout under the stairs leading to the shed, where the furry brood was nestled in a pile of dried-out leaves and twigs. The mother didn't appear to be feral; she was well-fed with a healthy gray coat. She was just a bit out of her element.

Just like Georgia.

Georgia had promised herself she would keep her phone confined in her aunt's old wooden bread box until at least 4 p.m. (happy hour—or not so happy, depending on what messages had come through in the meantime), but this was an emergency, right? What kind of person would she be, leaving those poor, defenseless animals out in the rain? Talk about bad press. And it wasn't like she was about to take them inside. Just the thought of vacuuming all that fur was all the permission she needed to free her phone. She'd braced herself for an onslaught of messages on her home screen, and was surprised to find that none had come through. Was she already irrelevant?

After a quick online search for the local animal shelter and a message left on their voicemail, Georgia had a purpose for the day. It wasn't glamorous, and it required her to drive in the rain, which she hated, but it was a welcome event; Georgia didn't do downtime. "Let's get you somewhere safe," she whispered to her box of kittens as she navigated around puddles to get to her car.

She placed the box in the backseat of her rented Audi, shut the back door, then paused. She opened the door again and strapped the seat belt across the box, congratulating herself on how well she was executing this small heroic act.

The GPS guided her the ten minutes it took to navigate the winding, tree-lined roads to reach the Sunset County Animal Shelter, where she planned to deliver her rescued strays then get back to the business of her day, which so far included waking up early after yet another terrible sleep, drinking too much coffee, resisting looking at the news, getting dressed and made up for no one, and looking out the window waiting for something to happen. The rest of the day promised more of the same, so really, this little adventure might be the highlight.

The shelter, a small limestone structure with a steep gabled roof, sat at the top of Sunset County's Main Street, which led down to the shore of Hollyberry Lake, one of the four sparkling lakes in the charming but very dead Northern Ontario town. Out front, a sprawling garden of mums in every shade of red, yellow and orange were like a mirror reflection of the large red maples flanking the building, their branches swaying in the breeze overhead. The sign outside needed a fresh coat of paint and the windows were on the dustier side, but for all its flaws it exuded the same homespun charm that oozed from every pore of Sunset County, a stark contrast to the traffic jams and bright lights awaiting Georgia's return to Los Angeles. Whenever that would be.

The mother cat eyed Georgia warily as she unbuckled the seat belt and gathered the banker's box in her arms. "Trust me, you're better off here," Georgia said as she kicked the back door closed with her boot. She scolded herself for forgetting the umbrella in the car as she turned toward the front entrance, eager to shield the little kittens from the rain. She was capable, sure. But no one would ever mistake her for the nurturing type.

As she let herself in through the front gate, a red van across the street caught her eye, emblazoned with a Channel 4 News logo. Georgia froze as she watched a petite woman with long braids emerge from the front seat, and a camera operator pull his gear out from the back of the truck. Impossible. How had they found her? No one was supposed to have the slightest clue who she was in this teeny-tiny town in the middle of nowhere. Wasn't that why she'd taken a five-hour flight and driven north, to the last place on earth she'd ever be recognized? She'd only been there three days, and had barely left Nina's cottage.

With her heart in her throat and the box in her hands, Georgia bolted up the path and let herself in through the shelter door, then peered out the window past the Help Wanted sign (Help wanted? More like help needed!). The camera operator was fiddling with the mic on the reporter's lapel. Georgia gasped, her mind racing. As if she hadn't suffered enough of an invasion of her privacy over the last few weeks.

She stared intently at the news crew across the street, then almost jumped out of her skin when she heard a throat clearing behind her. "Can I help you?" a voice sounded from what felt like inches away.

Georgia spun around, colliding with a woman, causing her to tip the box sideways. She felt the mother and babies slide to the side of the box, and narrowly saved them from tumbling out by quickly shifting her arm to block them. Before she could even look up at the source of her surprise, she felt the box level in her arms as the woman in front of her helped steady it. "Whoa, whoa," she said. "Easy there."

One of the little kittens, a miniature orange-and-white puffball the size of a teacup, had gotten loose and had its claws stuck in her sleeve. Georgia allowed the woman to take the box while she cupped the kitten in her hand, gently dislodging its teeny-tiny claws from the threads of her sweater.

"Nice save," the woman said. Georgia cradled the kitten in her hands, steadying herself, and took in the stranger in front of her, a woman with the most intense brown eyes she'd ever seen and perfect wavy chestnut hair that fell just above her shoulders. She wore a white lab coat over a hunter green sweater and jeans, and looked at Georgia with a curious and amused expression. She peered inside the box. "Ah. I see someone didn't heed public health advice."

Georgia narrowed her eyes. "Excuse me?" The kitten moved in her hand. She looked down at the baby animal, who rubbed its little head on her wrist, then yawned, revealing a pink tongue not much bigger than a pencil eraser.

"Looks like he likes you," said the woman, as the mother cat made a squawking mewing noise. "But Mom's not too happy."

"Here," Georgia said. She placed the kitten back in the box in the woman's arms and looked up at her. "So, here they are."

The woman raised her eyebrows.

"I left a message earlier?" Georgia said.

"Not that I know of," the woman said, looking back in the box. "Seamus isn't here right now. He's the manager. He would have told you that you have to keep them."

"Well, these aren't mine. I found them."

She looked at Georgia quizzically. "Found them?"

"Under the porch out back of my aunt's house. I don't live here. I mean, I'm just in town for a bit. I don't know who these belong to." For someone who coached others in speaking for a living, Georgia felt her speech getting all muddled up in the woman's deep brown gaze. "And why would you be surprised?" She looked around the room. "You're an animal shelter, right?"

The woman looked away, then furrowed her brow. Georgia followed her gaze out to the street where the news team was still standing and remembered why she'd flown in there like a tornado.

"We're currently an animal shelter. We might be without a home soon, though." She studied the reporters, then looked at Georgia. "The county's plans to cut funding were just announced yesterday, and our regular fundraising won't be enough to cover the shortfall. Looks like the local news is reporting on the story."

A wave of relief washed over Georgia. Of course there were things going on in the world other than her own personal, and very embarrassing, drama. For example, the undeniable electric charge pulsing through her from standing so close to this incredibly alluring woman. She steeled herself. If there was anything Georgia O'Neill was good at, it was keeping her cool. One recent lapse didn't negate that, right? "Okay, well, I'm very sorry to hear that, Doctor..."

"Melanie Carter. Mel. Don't apologize to me. I just check in on the animals once a week or so. It's my uncle Seamus who's losing. This place has been his life's work. Not to mention the animals." Mel was a tad cool in her demeanor, but at the mention of her uncle and the animals Georgia thought she detected her expression softening.

"I'm Georgia O'Neill. What will happen to them?" Georgia asked. She looked behind Mel's shoulder to see a hallway that led to a series of rooms where she guessed the animals were kept.

"Nothing's set in stone yet. But we'll try to move them to another place a few counties over. So," she said, looking down at the box of kittens, "we're in no place to take in any new animals."

"What am I supposed to do with these?" Georgia asked, straightening her posture. The kittens were cute. But seeing Mel Carter, with her broad shoulders and narrow waist that suggested a regular fitness regimen, holding on to the box, inspecting the contents—well, that just about made her knees buckle.

Georgia felt Mel's eyes studying her. Was she sizing up her ability to care for another living thing? Or was that flicker in her eye something else? Georgia was suddenly glad she'd taken the time to get herself together that morning rather than giving in to the temptation of spending the rest of her day in her pajamas. Being locked in Mel Carter's—*Doctor* Mel Carter's—gaze was poking some serious holes in her trademark cool confidence.

"You'll have to take them with you," Mel said, and for a moment Georgia wanted nothing more than for the doctor to lay out more orders. She'd pretty much do anything Mel wanted her to, and maybe then some. "There's really no—"

Mel was interrupted by the door to the shelter opening behind Georgia, and a small gray-haired man coming through the entrance. His glasses were crooked and the laces on one shoe were untied, though it was unclear as to whether his disheveled state was situational or just a general way of being. He bumbled past Georgia without acknowledging her. "Melanie," he said. "How's my Checkers?"

"Just fine, Seamus. I gave her a dose of vitamin E mixed with selenium. She should be back to her old self before you know it."

"Thank you, Doctor. Now what have we got here?" Georgia watched as Seamus peered into the box of kittens that she was apparently about to inherit. He let out a shout of glee. "It's Molly! Oh, the Harris family is going to be overjoyed. They've been worried sick about her. And look at these kittens. Beautiful."

Seamus turned and did a double take when he noticed Georgia. "Oh. Hello. Where did you find them? Not sure if you've noticed the posters all around town but there are two young girls who have been beside themselves for weeks. Seems that they'd been trying to keep her inside, with her delicate condition and all, but one of them left the back door open after burning a batch of sugar cookies and Ms. Molly here couldn't resist an adventure. She's an outdoor cat, but she must have been chased or scared by something and lost her way."

Lost her way. Georgia and Molly had more in common than she'd initially thought. She was about to answer, when Mel cut in. "Georgia here found them under her porch and wanted to dump them off," she said.

Georgia's face went hot. "I found them under my aunt's porch. And I wasn't dumping them off. It's an animal shelter."

Mel's expression changed from skeptical to amused. "You're right." She smiled, and Georgia instinctively touched her neck, something she'd trained her clients not to do. It showed vulnerability. Weakness. Which was what Mel was making her feel. Mel peered back in the box. "It's just frustrating how many people don't neuter or spay their cats and aren't willing to care for the kittens."

"The Harris family will take good care. Now, why don't I call them?" Seamus said. "Finally, some good news today." He pulled back the curtain to look at the news truck driving away.

"I heard you might be losing some funding," Georgia said. "I'm really sorry." She paused, looking back at the kittens still in Mel's arms, and again had to gather herself. Someone gorgeous holding kittens? Come on. They made calendars out of this, didn't they? "I'd be happy to deliver them to the family. My day's pretty open." Another task. She was starting to feel like herself again.

Seamus nodded. "Wonderful. I'll go call them now." He looked at Mel. "They live just up on Russell Road. You're heading that direction, right? Why don't you show Georgia the way there?"

"Happy to," Mel said, but Georgia failed to detect any happiness in her response.

"Thanks," said Georgia. Dropping off a lost cat and her kittens to a family who thought they were gone forever? If only she could get that news crew to come back to get some footage of this. And maybe a shot or two of the gorgeous vet cradling some very adorable animals.

She watched as Mel grabbed her jacket from behind the reception desk. This was supposed to be a break from work. But all of a sudden, Mel Carter had Georgia's mind on overdrive.

Mel knew very well she should have thanked Georgia. Probably profusely, for going out of her way like she did. Heck, she'd been in the business long enough to know that some people were downright cruel to animals. It tapped into an anger deep inside her that propelled her to go to work every day. Taking care of those animals that were turned away, who were so humble and so brave despite their circumstances. Nothing deserved her attention more than that.

She'd once thought of going into oncology, or even dentistry, but she thanked her lucky stars every day that she'd had the instinct to pursue veterinary medicine. There were lots of great humans, but there were lots of downright rotten ones too. Mel knew that well enough, and every day tried to silence the voice in her head that told her she attracted the bad ones. So, she was more than fine to devote 100 percent of her energy to those beings that were 100 percent deserving of all the attention and care in the world.

Mel had never seen this Georgia woman before. She'd grown up in Sunset County and knew the whole town, as well as the seasonal cottagers. Not only had she never seen or heard of her, but she stuck out in a way that was intriguing but set off more than one alarm bell. Firstly, her smooth skin had a hint of a summer glow that wasn't common in these parts toward the end of October. Then, there was the fairly impractical nature of her attire, which, granted, caused Mel's eyes to linger maybe a moment or two too long, but didn't align with the usual jeans and fleece pullovers sported by most in the area. Georgia appeared as though she'd stepped right out of the pages of one of those fashion magazines her sister, Andie, always had lying around her place, the ones Mel teased her for with their headlines of "How to Own It in the Bedroom and the Boardroom!" or "Get Clear Skin from the Inside Out!"

She held open the shelter door for Georgia, then followed her to the street. "You can follow me in your car. It's only a few minutes up the road." She looked at Georgia's Audi, which had a sticker from the car rental company on the bumper. "Hope you're not planning on staying in town too long. Those tires won't cut it up here once the snow comes."

Georgia fished her keys out of her purse. "The guy at the rental company told me they're 'all season.'"

Mel knew her last comment came across as unwelcoming. She'd been brought up better than that. "Where are you from?" she asked as Georgia unlocked her door and slid into the driver's seat. The car was definitely impractical. But she looked great behind the wheel.

"LA."

Now the tan made sense. "So, not much experience with winter."

"Actually, I grew up right outside of Chicago. I know the drill. I'll be gone by the time the bad weather comes." She flashed Mel a quick smile.

So she was just passing through. Most Sunset

County cottagers came from Toronto, but every now and then someone visited from farther afield. "That's me," Mel said, nodding to her silver pickup truck. "I'll lead the way."

Through her rearview mirror as she buckled her seat belt, Mel watched as Georgia applied lipstick, for whatever reason, and ran her hand through her silky, toffee-colored hair. Mel cleared her throat and shook her head. She'd lead Georgia to the Harris place and then be on her way. One thing Mel had always shared with animals was a strong sense of instinct. And her instinct was telling her that Georgia might be drop-dead gorgeous, but she was trouble. And when it came to fight, flight or freeze, Mel knew enough by this time in her life that flight left you with fewer problems in the long run.

She guided Georgia through the winding roads just outside of the Sunset County downtown, then pulled into the long gravel driveway leading to the Harris home. The family, clearly having received Seamus's call, were all assembled on the front porch, waiting to welcome home their cherished pet. Hopefully they'd be ready to house six more. Mel slowed to a stop at the side of the driveway, and rolled down her window as Georgia pulled up beside her.

"Here we are," Mel said. "Take care."

"What, you're not coming up?" Georgia asked. "What if they have any questions? I have absolutely no idea how to care for kittens."

Mel considered. Georgia was right. She sighed, then shifted back into Drive. She'd stay for a few minutes to make sure the family was all set up to care for their new pets, then head back to her clinic in town to finish the pile of paperwork waiting for her. A tall, boring pile of paperwork. It felt like exactly the solution to how hyperaware she'd been feeling since Georgia O'Neill burst through the doors of the shelter, her magnetic energy awakening something in her that Mel had worked to stow away for the past three years. Ever since everything she believed in and the life she thought was a happy one turned out to be a complete sham. She had to get away from Georgia, despite a nagging desire to be closer to her side.

Mel navigated the rest of the way up the path to the house. The two little girls were jumping up and down on the front porch, huge grins on their faces. She sat for a moment, watching as Georgia removed the box from her backseat—did she have a seat belt around it?—then proudly handed the box over to the girls, who at their parents' permission had run down from the porch, almost attacking Georgia. It was a pretty great scene. Mel struggled to keep herself from grinning, then got out of her truck.

"Molly!" the younger girl said, hoisting the mother cat out of the box and into her arms, as the other twin enveloped them both in a giant hug. "We thought you were gone forever."

One of the girls separated herself from the hug

and peered into the box. "Mommy, Daddy, look at the kittens! They're so cute!" she exclaimed, carefully lifting one out of the box. "We're keeping them, right?"

"We'll see," said the dad. "Seven is a lot of cats in one house."

"Might be a bylaw infraction," Mel said. Georgia shot her a look. Well, someone had to be the practical one, right?

"I'm sure we can find a home for a few of these cuties," Mrs. Harris said, peering into the box. "We can't thank you enough for finding Molly. There've been a lot of tears around here."

"I'm just glad she found her way home," Georgia said, her eyes sparkling. Mel swallowed hard as Georgia trailed her hand through her hair, allowing it to cascade down her back in a perfect thickness that Mel could easily imagine running her fingers through.

Georgia reached in and picked up the same orange-and-white kitten that had gotten stuck in her sweater earlier. "You're home, little one," she cooed, nuzzling the miniature animal against her face. Mel breathed in sharply at the idea of touching her perfect, tanned skin. It was time to leave.

"He likes you," said one of the little girls to Georgia.

"Let us know if you want dibs on him. You can visit in the meantime," their dad said.

Georgia laughed. "Oh, not me. I'm just in town for a bit. Good luck finding homes for them, though."

After another minute of small talk and thank-yous, and a few instructions for care from Mel, the family waved goodbye and carried the box into their home, leaving Mel and Georgia standing outside together.

"There you go. Your noble deed for the day," Mel said. "Collecting some good karma."

"Ha!" Georgia said, rolling her eyes. "Don't I need it."

Mel didn't know what that meant, and had no intention of probing, but it confirmed her instincts about Georgia O'Neill. *Trouble.*

"Alright, well, you enjoy your time with your aunt," Mel said, turning toward her truck.

"Actually, she passed last month. I'm just here— well, I'm helping sort a couple of things out with her estate."

Mel turned back. "Nanny?" she asked.

Georgia looked confused. "Her name was Nina. Nina Miller."

"We all—" Mel took a moment to gather herself. "Everyone in town called her Nanny. She was like everyone's grandma."

"I didn't know that." She looked to the side when she said it. Had Georgia and her aunt been close? Maybe she just wasn't telling the truth. Mel had never been good at detecting a lie, a crucial flaw that had only resulted in her getting burned. Torched, actually.

Georgia's eyes flickered with sadness, and Mel softened. "Well, I'm sorry about your aunt. She was an amazing woman." Georgia's eyes welled up a bit. Mel had to get out of there. "Lots of helpful people in this town if you need anything." It was the truth. Mel had only left Sunset County for a while to go to university and then vet school, and the familiar workings of the small town, and the way people took care of one another, were close to Mel's heart.

Georgia was quiet, and Mel felt the pressure of her waiting for a better response, but she said nothing. She might have been raised to be polite, but she was no therapist.

"Okay, well, thanks for bringing me out here," Georgia said. "Good luck with the rest of the animals at the shelter." Once again, Mel felt the strong pull of the vulnerability that was showing through the cracks of Georgia's confident, self-assured presentation. She watched as Georgia got in her car, and Mel returned the quick wave she offered as she drove away.

Mel heaved a big sigh as she got back into her truck, forcing herself to relax. But the way she was feeling? It might take a bit more than some deep breathing to recover from being around Georgia. She was a spark. The type that Mel knew could blur her judgment.

If Mel had learned anything in the past few years, it was that there were all sorts of ways that life could pull the rug out from under you. And she needed to stay on solid ground.

Chapter Two

A small package was propped up at the door on the front porch of Aunt Nina's cottage. It could only be from one person. Despite Georgia's desire to remain as under the radar as possible for the next few weeks, she thought it prudent to let at least her best friend, Paulina, under strict secrecy, know the exact location of her hideout lest some terrible accident befall her.

So far, so good. She hadn't counted on being a hero in her first few days in town, but she had to admit she'd enjoyed seeing the looks on the young girls' faces when she'd returned Molly and the kittens.

And then there was Mel Carter. The veterinarian looked as though she'd walked out of a casting call for the role, every bit the "I'm not a doctor but I play one on TV" stereotype. Seriously. The woman was a knockout, and it irritated Georgia to no end that her attempt to do a good deed went so unnoticed. Punished, even! That comment about her being too irresponsible to neuter her cat? If it weren't for her disarming, penetrating gaze, and the subtle swagger of her detached demeanor, Georgia might have had the wherewithal to bite back. It was a capacity that she was rarely without.

She sighed, picked up the package and brought it into the redwood-shingled cottage her aunt had lived in for the last thirty years, the one she'd left behind every time she'd traveled to visit Georgia and her parents in San Diego in Georgia's early childhood, or Evanston in her teens. Georgia's calendar had never afforded her the time off to travel to Nina's place, when summer enrichment programs, SAT prep and competitive tennis all began to take over her life, all in the name of following the carefully laid-out path her parents had designed for her. But she'd loved when her aunt visited. Nina was younger than her sister, Georgia's mother, by ten years, and took an interest in Georgia's life beyond her schoolwork and extracurricular achievements. A visit from Nina always promised frivolous fun, like trips to the soft-serve ice cream truck in town for breakfast, or hours-long games of Monopoly. Georgia could only imagine that there were some negotiations behind-the-scenes and some disapproval from her parents, who only put up with Nina's disregard for

Georgia's usual routines because it allowed them to leave on research field trips without too much guilt.

Standing in the entrance of Nina's cottage, she felt the same sense of calm that her aunt had brought to any space she entered. It was a small structure, but immaculately maintained. The wood-paneled living room looked out over a small, tree-lined inlet of Robescarres Lake, which afforded some privacy from the passing speedboats, canoes and kayaks. A bedroom sat to the left side of the living room, and to the right of the entrance was a small, bright kitchen edged with countertops that offered forest views wherever you were cooking.

So they called her Nanny. The fact that Mel knew her aunt wasn't surprising—Nina was very social, and could barely walk ten meters down the street without striking up a casual conversation with whoever happened to be walking by—but the way that Mel dropped her aunt's nickname so casually, as though Georgia should have known, summoned a lump in her throat that she was having a tough time swallowing.

She plopped down into the worn green corduroy couch that wasn't about to win any design awards, but felt like a perfect hug—the kind of couch you could spend a whole day on, reading paperback mysteries and drinking hot chocolate. She examined the box in her hands, laughing to herself at the name Paulina had addressed the box to: "Hurricane Georgia." Only Paulina could get away with that. With anyone else, it would be too soon.

Georgia winced when she recalled, for the millionth time, the event that had earned her that nickname. How could a mere thirty seconds threaten to tear down everything she'd worked for all these years? How long would she be the laughingstock of the industry, the bringer of the greatest irony: the PR rep who earned the worst PR of all time?

It had all happened three weeks earlier. Georgia had known the red-carpet gala fundraiser would be a challenging evening, but thought she could manage. Days before the event, she'd received notice that Nina had finally lost her battle with cancer. And that there were strict instructions that she didn't want any kind of funeral or end-of-life celebration. Georgia was grieving, hard, crumbling inside but doing everything in her power to hold it together for her job. She'd always been able to compartmentalize.

What she hadn't anticipated was the combination of that grief paired with the incredible amount of pressure she'd been feeling in the first three months of her new role as Brand Reputation and Issues Response Specialist at Herstein PR, one of the world's leading agencies—with offices in LA, London, Miami, Toronto and New York—and the company to which she'd committed every last ounce of her time and energy over the past several years.

Not only was Georgia starting to handle the major

flubs of some of the firm's top clients, but by special request, she'd continued to rep a huge tennis star who loved Georgia and insisted she'd employ another firm if Georgia wasn't on her team. The athlete was one of the marquee guests of the charity event that evening. Georgia was accompanying her on the red carpet, and stuck by her side during interview after interview until one of the journalists had veered off of the agreed-upon script. Instead of being asked about her athletic prowess and many amazing achievements, both on the court and in her philanthropic work, the star athlete was questioned about her love life and her weight, which had recently gone up and was the subject of massive tabloid speculation—was she pregnant? Was she not? Georgia knew very well that she was not, and had been scrambling to figure out how to shut down the interview without causing a scene.

The pivotal moment came when the journalist asked an even more insulting question, insinuating that the tennis star's weight was the reason behind her recent catastrophic loss in the finals of the US Open.

Georgia didn't remember much, but the videos that went viral on social media immediately following the event quite easily filled in the memory gaps. Georgia first used her elbow to jostle the tennis star out of the way, preventing her from answering the question. Not only did she then proceed to give the reporter a piece of her mind (filled with expletives that Georgia had no idea were part of her vernacular), but in her expressive delivery she sent the tennis star's glass of red wine flying toward the journalist, who, as it turned out, was a former college badminton player and boasted tremendous reflexes, the type that allowed him to duck prior to being hit by the projectile refreshment.

As luck would have it, the multiple-Academy-Award-winning starlet who was hosting the event, Aurelia Martin, was wearing a stunning white Valentino gown and happened to be directly behind the journalist, engaged in an interview of her own, and was splattered from cheek to hip with Georgia's assault. And it was all. On. Video. From multiple angles. In a way that allowed news outlets to create a humiliating, almost 360-degree compilation of the footage, which then traveled to TikTok and Instagram and beyond, where millions of people had viewed the dramatic event, and Georgia's complete and utter humiliation.

And then there were the memes. Objectively, some of them were quite clever, and if Georgia hadn't been the subject of the jokes, she might have admired the tidal wave of fun at her expense. She'd always been in awe of the power of social media.

Her meltdown had resulted in the VP of the company mandating that Georgia take a "wellness pause" from her work. Once she'd wrapped her head around the forced exile, and the impact on what, until recently, had been a promising career trajectory, Georgia weighed her options. The company owned a villa in the Turks and Caicos but the island would be teeming with their clients on holidays. She briefly toyed with the idea of one of those silent retreats in Colorado, or even just hiding under her duvet for a good long while, but when she received the call from the lawyer handling her aunt's estate, informing her that Nina had left everything to her, hiding out in the small Canadian town felt like the perfect move.

Her aunt wouldn't be there, but maybe being in her home, surrounded by her things, would give Georgia the assurance and guidance she needed to get back on her feet and recover from this fiasco. Nina had always been her guide, and as gutted as Georgia was that she was no longer there to lean on, she longed to at least feel her spirit. Not to mention that handling her aunt's estate would give her something productive to work on, even though in typical Nina style, everything was so well organized, and her place was so tidy and clutter-free, that there really wasn't much to do.

Georgia's parents, as always, were off in some far-flung location—was it Krabi province in Thailand this time?—conducting research on infectious disease ecology and evolution, and were happy to leave the task to their only child, who had seemed to gravitate to Nina more than them, anyway.

Georgia's goal was to get the cottage on the market in the next week, in the sweet spot before the fall ended and the beginning of what she'd read was a slow winter real estate market in Sunset County. By then, she'd be welcomed back to the office and could pick up where she'd left off, helping the brightest stars and athletes in LA manage their public personas.

She picked up the box she'd found on the front porch, peeled back the packing tape, then laughed as she opened the top flap to reveal the contents. Paulina knew her well. Nestled into some shredded paper threads was a bottle of her favorite red wine from the vineyard they loved in Sonoma, as well as a jar of Dr. Barbara Sturm face mask, a pair of furry hot pink Gucci slippers and a note reading "Hope you find your zen place! xoxo—P."

She instinctively reached for her phone to text her friend and remembered that she had returned it to the bread box and vowed to keep it shut away until 4 p.m.

It was only one thirty.

Georgia contemplated the living room of the cottage, trying to decide her next move. She needed to do a bit of staging before putting the cottage on the market, but that could wait.

The energy that she'd been feeling since being in the presence of Mel Carter hadn't gone anywhere, and one of the first things she planned on doing once she freed her phone was going to be looking her up on the internet to see what she could find. Despite Mel's less-than-perfect manners, Georgia predicted she'd have a squeaky-clean online presence. But Georgia had a few more tricks up her sleeve, with a forensic accountant's level of scrutiny from working with her clients.

If anything, she could spend a few minutes studying any profile pictures she came across. Her pink lips. Those deep brown eyes that could make you forget it was a human necessity to breathe, and the easy way she tucked her dark, glossy waves behind her ear. Georgia shivered.

She had some serious energy to expend.

After changing into her running gear, she did a few stretches then set out to the backcountry roads around Nina's cottage. She settled into a comfortable pace, inhaling the cool fall air that carried a faint hint of bonfire smoke but felt cleaner than any air she'd ever breathed. Georgia was used to hills near her place in Hollywood and found a sudden burst of energy that she gave in to, finally settling into her favorite part about jogging: the moment when her mind went completely blank, and her only focus was getting to the next imaginary goalpost she set for herself on the path ahead.

The roads on the outskirts of Sunset County had a wide gravel shoulder on each side, so Georgia felt safe even when the occasional car or motorcycle whizzed by. Every time a nagging thought or a flash to the last few weeks threatened to enter her consciousness, Georgia picked up the pace just a bit more, and the increased challenge helped to keep the intrusions at bay.

Her watch alerted her that she'd hit the five-kilometer mark. She slowed to a walk in front of a unique, modern-looking home that was a touch out of place compared to the other houses and cottages in the area. The wide glass windows reflected the trees around it in a way that allowed the forest to continue uninterrupted, as though the house was trying to camouflage itself.

She'd stopped to examine the building further when a big fluffy dog with black, white and golden fur came bounding across the yard to greet her at the fence. Georgia crouched down and extended her hand through an opening between the fence posts, allowing the dog to sniff her, then she petted its soft head. Seemed she was becoming quite the animal whisperer.

"What's your name?" Georgia asked quietly, as the dog panted and licked her hands. The dog had the gentlest eyes she'd ever seen, as though it could peer right into someone's soul. The earnest, sweet animal in front of her gave her a small window into why people loved being in the presence of dogs.

Then again, they didn't necessarily smell terrific.

"I didn't peg you as an animal person," a voice called from closer to the house. A familiar voice, which was unusual in an unfamiliar town.

Georgia stood up, and her heart, which had just started to slow down in the brief break from running, immediately sped up again at the sight of Mel Carter, who was emerging from the front entrance of the house holding a dog leash and making her way toward Georgia. A hot blush burned her already red cheeks. "You live here?" Georgia asked. "Nice place."

"You seem surprised," Mel said, her eyes traveling over Georgia's tight running top and pants, sending a heat wave of desire coursing through her body as though Mel's gaze was a laser beam. Mel had also changed since Georgia had last seen her and was still wearing her faded jeans, but she'd swapped out her lab coat for a red-and-black houndstooth wool button up, rolled up at the sleeves.

Georgia had to consciously resist the urge to touch her neck, or fix her shirt, or smooth her hair. "Well, it's a bit surprising. I mean, not that you live here. Just that of all the places in the area I could have stopped for a break in front of—"

"Franny here has that effect on people," Mel said, opening the gate and leashing up Franny before she could bound toward Georgia. "She's a bit of a neighborhood ambassador."

"She's very cute," Georgia said, taking a tentative step forward to pet Franny again. Franny leaped up, trying desperately to lick her cheek. Georgia laughed and scratched the dog behind her ears when she settled down. "Rescue, I'm assuming?"

"Yeah," said Mel. She squatted down to Franny's height, and immediately Franny turned back to Mel for more pets. "She's a Bernese mountain dog. A farmer down the road got really badly injured in a trailer accident. He's not walking anymore, so he had to give up the farm. I took her in a couple years ago." Mel stood up, and Franny immediately jumped up again, almost hugging her, then licked her cheek. "Okay, okay," she said. "We're going for a walk. Don't worry." She looked at Georgia. "So—how's it going at your aunt's place? I'm sure that's a big chore. Going through everything."

Georgia nodded. "Luckily she was a minimalist. And a bit of a neat freak. So, it's really not a lot of work. Just—" Despite herself, she found the words coming out of her mouth. "Just a bit hard to say good-bye. We were close."

Mel's expression softened, telling Georgia that she knew something about her pain. And for a moment, Georgia saw an opening, as though Mel was about to offer her help. Or invite her to walk together. There was a shimmer of warmth, a genuine connection.

"Well, good luck with everything. Let's go, Franny," Mel said, taking a step away from her, and suddenly the spell was broken and Georgia felt foolish for entertaining the idea that a woman she had met mere hours ago would have any interest in doing anything to help her. "You know your way home, right?"

"Yeah, for sure," Georgia said, adjusting her watch. Had she done something wrong? She knew some people didn't like to talk about death, but surely someone in the health-care profession would know very well that it was a fact of life, wouldn't they? And what about that current of electricity between them? There was no way Mel didn't feel it too.

She glanced over her shoulder to check the road before crossing and gave a quick wave before resuming her jog, but Mel had already turned her back and was walking the other way. "Take care," Mel called, without turning around.

Georgia stared for a moment, then started back toward Nina's cottage. Mel had clearly missed the class on bedside manners at vet school.

Try as she might to get back into the same zone she'd found so effortlessly at the beginning of her run, Georgia had no luck. That look in Mel's eyes—the one that for the very briefest of moments made Georgia desperate to know what she was thinking—was burned in her brain, and no amount of pushing herself and letting the fatigue overtake her would make it go away.

She'd come to Sunset County seeking a quiet place to hide out while she settled her aunt's affairs, and where she could find some way back to being the woman she was: a kick-ass PR agent, on top of her game. An achiever. A woman who could hold it together in the most challenging of situations.

So far, Mel Carter and her strong frame, and her deep, penetrating eyes, were *not* helpful in this endeavor.

Not one bit.

* * *

As soon as Mel knew Georgia was long gone, back toward Robescarres Lake, she stopped for a moment and took a deep breath while Franny sniffed a fallen branch at the side of the road. She looked out into the thick forest to her right and shook her head.

She knew she'd been incredibly rude. And should have asked Georgia if she needed anything. Her aunt had just died, an aunt she was close to, and now she had to pack up her place. Of course, that would be a hard thing to do. Heck, extending a hand, even to a stranger, was the essence of living in a small town, and she'd had more than her share of offers to help after everything that had happened to her three years ago. Not that she'd asked for it, but there was something reassuring in knowing there were good people looking out for you.

Even knowing this, she couldn't bring herself to do it. Because as soon as Mel offered help, and as soon as Georgia said yes, well, then she was in trouble. Georgia O'Neill was the first woman since Breanne who'd made Mel feel as though she was no longer standing on solid ground. She'd given in to that feeling for Breanne, big-time, and was still raw from the ache of that loss. A loss on two counts, and it was sometimes hard to know which was worse.

In the first few days, it was Breanne's death. The agony of losing the woman she loved and the future she'd envisioned, a future that was so vivid and so promising that it seemed impossible that something so alive and real could be snuffed out in a moment.

And then, the details of the car accident were confirmed, and her best friend since childhood came clean with what was going on. Mel learned the reason why Breanne was rushing to get home, on a rainy night, when the roads were slippery. Mel had called her to say she'd just landed a day early from a conference and was going to take her out for dinner. Knowing the truth turned her sorrow, which was infused with a deep disappointment, into fierce anger.

Instead of going home from the airport, Mel had traveled by taxi to the hospital, where Breanne was about to take her last breath. Mel would never forget running through the hallways of the ICU ward, dodging wheelchairs and beds and nurses muttering at her to slow down, moments away from getting to the love of her life, with her suitcase trailing behind her and a ring in her pocket.

She'd missed saying goodbye.

It hadn't even for a moment struck her as strange that her best friend, Lauren, was there. Given what they'd been through together growing up, from skinned knees, soccer championships and failed math tests as kids, to supporting Lauren through her mother's Parkinson's disease and Lauren seeing Mel through the stress of vet school, of course she'd be there when Mel needed her most.

It was days later, over a bottle of whiskey, in a

moment when she felt like she had her best friend, basically her sister, by her side to help her through what would be an impossible road ahead, when Mel learned the truth.

Lauren had called on the way over. "Can we talk?" she'd said. Her voice was timid, restrained. Nothing like her usual easygoing, affable self.

"Yeah, sure," Mel had said, not in the mood for conversation but grateful for her friend's company. She was working on her speaking notes for Breanne's celebration of life, and was terrified by the idea of standing up in front of a crowd and trying to make it through the speech without losing it.

When she opened the door, Lauren stood holding a bottle of Jim Beam, dark circles under her teary eyes, which were avoiding any contact with Mel's.

Mel had pulled two rocks glasses from the cupboard and poured them each a measure. "I might need you up there with me," she said. "In case I can't make it all the way through."

When she'd turned back to look at Lauren, her head was in her hands, her body shaking with guttural sobs. "I'm sorry. Oh, god, Mel, I hate myself."

Without Lauren even saying another word, the pieces of the puzzle started to click together. They'd always gotten along well when the three of them hung out, which Mel loved. Lauren would sometimes bring dates when they went out for drinks or to the movies, but she'd never suspected that the easy banter and affection between Lauren and Breanne was anything more than her girlfriend and her best friend getting along well for her sake.

"It just...happened," Lauren had whispered.

Just *happened*. Like the sunrise. Like the tide going out. Like a sneeze you couldn't control. Mel's stomach lurched, her anger clouding and shaking her vision at the same time.

She sat stiff and humiliated as Lauren choked out the hideous details of the affair. It had started during the trip the three of them had planned to take to Algonquin Park. Mel came down with strep throat the day they were supposed to leave. She'd encouraged them to go on without her. Then Mel's late nights getting the clinic up and running had apparently facilitated future meetups. She listened as Lauren tried to absolve herself of her guilt. *We felt so terrible. We were planning to tell you the truth*. And again: *It just* happened.

When she'd looked down at the table in front of her, she could barely make out the jotted-down notes she'd been working on of ideas for what she was going to say about Breanne. The words staring back at her rearranged themselves, accusing her of being a complete fool. "How could you?" she managed.

Lauren continued to sob silently.

Minutes passed as Mel let the truth sink in. "Leave," was all she could think of to say. It was the last word she'd ever said to Lauren.

Her life had seemed perfect. Then the person who mattered to Mel the most was gone, and the other, while still alive, was dead to her. Lauren had begged for her forgiveness, and in the weeks that followed, persisted in trying to convince Mel that their friendship could be mended. It took a while, but Lauren finally relented.

Over the past three years, the pain and anger had gradually turned to resignation, and a commitment to never get duped again. She'd tried therapy, but there didn't seem to be much of a point. It couldn't help her go back in time.

Small-town life suited her. She had a purpose, people knew her enough to respect that she liked to keep a polite distance, and there was the steadiness that very little changed, save for the cottagers and the weekenders passing through—mostly couples on a short getaway.

It had been a long time since she'd faced that same feeling she'd experienced when she first met Breanne on their university campus, when life seemed kind and it was conceivable that she could be happy. And although Mel knew nothing about Georgia O'Neill, how long she'd be in town for or what that meant for her, that familiar feeling was undeniable and set off every signal in her body to get as far away from Georgia as possible, as quickly as possible. Georgia thinking Mel was rude was way better than the alternative.

Franny sniffed, and Mel realized she'd been standing still for several minutes, staring out into the crimson-and-amber tapestry of the forest. "Come on," she called, then whistled, which made Franny leap up, wagging her tail in a fit of excitement.

Mel let Franny off her leash and watched her bound down the forest trail chasing a chipmunk, blissfully living in the moment. Animals were simple. Uncomplicated. They gave you all their love, unconditionally, and wanted nothing in return.

But most of all, they were loyal.

Chapter Three

"Hurricane Georgia, huh?" Georgia said, flopping back onto the couch with her phone.

Paulina's big grin filled the phone screen, and her booming laugh rang through the speaker. The sight of her best friend immediately brought up Georgia's spirits. Paulina was wearing a fluorescent yellow button-up with a black lightning bolt print and sparkly red-rimmed glasses, which fit her self-described "fabulous Indian Ms. Frizzle" aesthetic. "Come on. That was at least a category four," Paulina said.

"With the wreckage of a five. How are you?"

"Oh, you know. Grant's on the road right now. So I'm sleeping really well."

Georgia rolled her eyes, laughing. Paulina was in a new relationship with a semi-pro basketball player and loved to brag about his stamina, both on and off the court. "Miss you, though," Paulina said. "How are things there?"

"Well. I just finished organizing the apps on my phone by color, and I've watched at least two hours of dance videos on TikTok, so safe to say you might need to get up here ASAP."

"Wait, so what you're saying is you're actually taking a break?"

Georgia tilted the phone down so Paulina could see her outfit, a purple tie-dyed lounge set.

"Wait," Paulina said, "are you still in your pajamas? This is bad. I'm on my way."

"Yeah, right," Georgia said. As a senior associate at her law firm on a fast track to partner, Paulina was just as devoted to her job as Georgia. "It's been alright. I'm just... I'm restless." Georgia sighed and stared out the window to the lake, which was sparkling in the early evening light. Two loons bobbed close to shore, slowly paddling through the green lily pads dotting the surface of the water. At least she wasn't the only one in town with nothing to do.

"You're a workaholic. Makes sense. But you need this time."

"I'm not a workaholic."

"And I'm not a coffee addict."

"Fine. I'm finding it a bit challenging. But these slippers are definitely helping." Georgia pointed her feet in the air and wiggled her toes.

"Why don't you sign up for an online course or something? You've always talked about learning Mandarin."

"Nah."

"Scrapbooking?"

"Stop."

"Part-time job?"

"Ha. I might be needing one. Maybe I'll update my résumé."

"Volunteer? I know you love to work. But what about putting in some hours somewhere, just because it's a good thing to do? And good for your mental health."

"Maybe. Anyway, thanks for calling. I'm going to go organize my cosmetics bag or something. I'll call you tomorrow."

"Don't forget to relax. Miss you!"

Georgia tossed her phone on the coffee table and stared up at the ceiling. Where had she put that wine Paulina sent?

After pouring herself a generous glass of cabernet sauvignon (she was here to relax, wasn't she?) Georgia threw a couple of logs on the fire and sat back in front of the crackling flames, the light and heat comforting her while the pink evening sky began to fade to dark.

Maybe Paulina was onto something. She didn't need a work visa to volunteer. And doing something productive that contributed to society would look really good to her bosses and show them she was ready and able to work again. Maybe she could volunteer at Nina's old school. She could handle a few hours of playing with kids, couldn't she? Entertain them with a few celeb stories?

A quick Google search of the school board's website quashed that idea. All volunteers were required to provide a vulnerable sector check, which would take time to come through.

Maybe there was some kind of charity race or big event in the area she could help promote. Another few minutes of Google searching revealed a fundraising bingo that was happening at the local Legion, but it was scheduled for that evening.

Georgia sipped her wine. She'd figure this out.

Ever since she was a child, she'd been trained to be calculated and confident in everything she did, every decision she made. She was the one friends came to for advice. Other parents used her as an example for their own children: "Why can't you be more like that Georgia O'Neill?" She wore it as a badge of honor. And lived in a state of perpetual fear that the badge could be stripped away at any moment.

The truth was, Georgia liked being on top. She loved working hard, and her parents might have laid out the expectations, but Georgia happily met them.

It wasn't until she was in her first year at university that she felt the full weight of her parents' grand plan, each step in her life carefully mapped out for her, likely before she was even born.

College prep school. Violin lessons. Summer enrichment programs at campuses across the country. An exchange in Spain. And right into pre-med at Northwestern, where her parents were professors and researchers and could meticulously advise her on her course selections, professors most likely to write her a glowing reference for med school, and volunteer jobs and research positions at Chicago's top hospitals.

A bigger curveball had likely never been thrown their way when without telling them, Georgia had switched into modern languages with a minor in art history early in her second year. Georgia wasn't sure what had surprised them more: the one-eighty on her academic plan or her bringing home her first girlfriend at Thanksgiving.

And as always, Nina had been there to guide her through, taking her phone calls late into the night, talking for hours and helping her figure out the right thing to do. Not right for anyone else, but right for her and her alone.

And here she was, at a time when she should have been working to advance her career righting *other people's* wrongs, trying to figure out how to wipe her own slate clean and get back to the steady trajectory of success that was true to her heart and that she'd set in motion years ago.

Paulina was right. She should take this time here, in Sunset County, to rest and move beyond what had happened. It was a small part of her story, and it was time to get over it. She remembered that morning, when she'd thought the news truck was following her. When she'd peered out the shelter's window, past the Help Wanted sign.

The Help Wanted sign.

If there was anything the past twelve hours had taught Georgia, it was that she was an unexpected hit with animals. And how hard could it be, petting and cuddling kittens and puppies, racking up some volunteer hours and making a few well-curated social media posts that her bosses would hopefully see?

The shelter manager—what was his name? Samuel? Steven? Seamus. He seemed like a nice man. And someone who likely hadn't seen her video.

And then there was Mel Carter. She had to admit that the idea of seeing Mel again wasn't an entirely unpleasant one, even if she seemed a bit odd and prickly.

Either way, she could put up with Mel and her moods. Plus, she'd told Georgia she only worked there once a week.

She scrolled back in her call history and dialed the shelter's number. It was past business hours, so she left a voicemail. "Hello, Seamus, we met this morning," Georgia said. "Georgia O'Neill. I saw your Help Wanted sign when I came by with the kittens. And I'm ready to help." She concluded the message with her phone number and a promise to follow up if she didn't hear from him by noon the next day. It was always good practice to exert a little control over the situation.

Her dampened mood was slightly lifted by the idea of having something productive to do (the wine didn't hurt), and she sat back on the couch, watching the dancing flames in the fireplace and for the first time since arriving in Sunset County, she felt something approaching relaxation.

It was so quiet at Nina's place, and so warm and comforting. No wonder her aunt was always calm.

She'd lock in the volunteer job in the morning, and then do some work organizing her aunt's things later in the day. For now, she was going to enjoy the moment.

Right after she did some internet searching for Dr. Mel Carter.

"You mean that woman who was in here yesterday? Who's clearly never held an animal in her life, never mind has no experience whatsoever?" Mel said, moments after Seamus shared that he'd hired a new volunteer, and she'd be coming by momentarily to fill out the volunteer information form. Through gritted teeth, Mel was trying to manage her tone; she hated speaking to her gentle and kind uncle in a confrontational way.

"We've had that sign up for weeks, and no luck," Seamus said. "My back is giving me so much trouble, I can't keep up with all the extra work. And she seems nice."

Mel clenched her jaw. How was it that the one person she was eager to avoid was now about to invade her workspace? To be fair, most of Mel's time was spent at her clinic down the street, but still. What was Georgia up to? She was supposed to be dealing with her aunt's estate, not volunteering on a whim to make Mel's days more difficult.

"Fine." Mel sighed. "Hope she knows what she's getting into, though. It's not glamorous work. And she seems a bit—" she thought about the sheen in Georgia's thick, shiny hair, the expensive-looking outfit she'd worn to the shelter, the pristine Audi "—high maintenance."

"I'll give her the benefit of the doubt. It's not like anyone else is knocking down the door to help out."

Before Mel could respond, the door of the shelter flung open, and in strode Georgia, looking like a complete knockout in a pair of royal blue high-heeled shoes, a black leather jacket and oversize tortoiseshell sunglasses. Mel's annoyance melted away, and she steadied herself.

Georgia removed her sunglasses, revealing her hazel eyes framed with long lashes—eyes like a doe, but Mel wasn't sure she had the animal's trademark innocence.

"Georgia, welcome," Seamus said, rushing to the door to greet her and shake her hand. "We're so happy that you're interested in helping us out." Seamus looked at Mel expectantly.

Mel cleared her throat, trying to recover from Georgia's sparkling entrance, which had all but bowled her over. "Hey, Georgia," was all she could muster.

Georgia didn't seem fazed. "I printed out the volunteer form at my aunt's place. So, here it is. All filled out." She grinned and passed the paper to Seamus.

"Thank you," Seamus said, surveying the form. "Now, let me just pop this in a file folder, then I'll give you a tour of the facility."

Mel saw her chance to make an exit. "Alright then, I'll see you around," she said, and turned to her uncle. "I'll be back on Thursday. Just call if you need anything." She watched Seamus stand up on a chair to open the top cabinet, then stop, bending over and crying out in pain.

"You okay?" Mel asked, rushing to Seamus's side.

"My back," Seamus said, groaning, then accepted Mel's hand to help him off the chair. "I've really got to get to the chiropractor."

"Slowly, slowly," Mel said as Seamus got back on solid ground, wincing and holding his lower back.

"Can I call someone for you?" said Georgia, her big eyes shining with concern. She was right there with Mel, holding Seamus's other hand.

"No, no, I just need to rest for a few minutes," he said. With both of their assistance, he sank into the office chair, then looked at Georgia. "This is why we need you here. I'm getting too old to manage things on my own." Mel bristled.

"Well, I'm glad to be of service," Georgia said.

"Melanie, you don't mind giving Georgia a quick tour of the facility before you leave, do you?"

Mind? Of course she minded. Every moment she spent in Georgia's presence was another moment she felt herself losing her bearings. The woman was bewitching.

"I can come back tomorrow, if you're busy..." Georgia said, and Mel saw an out, until she looked down at Seamus's expectant expression. The old man knew her all too well.

"Not at all," Mel said through gritted teeth. Fine. The universe was testing her. She'd take Georgia on a quick tour, make sure Seamus was okay to get home on his own, then get the heck out of there.

She glanced at Georgia's impractical, albeit incredibly sexy footwear. Was she trying to torture her? "Have you got any other shoes you can wear? A number of our animals are out back. It's dirty."

"Ugh, what was I thinking?" Georgia laughed. "Sorry. In my line of work, heels are pretty much the uniform. I'm sure I'll be fine."

Despite herself, Mel couldn't help but smile. This would be interesting. What line of work did she mean? Cocktail waitress? Runway model? Pageant queen? Not that Mel was a fashion expert, but in her mind, any job that required a woman to wear heels was woefully behind the times. And Georgia O'Neill didn't seem like the kind of woman to be coerced into doing anything she didn't want to. So, the heels had to be a matter of personal preference.

"Alright. Follow me," Mel said, leading Georgia down the bright hallway toward the back room. Time to see how she'd do with their resident reptiles. "Right in here," she said, motioning to the open door at the end of the hall. "After you."

Heels clicking against the linoleum, Georgia breezed by, leaving the floral scent of her shampoo in her wake and causing Mel to take a deep breath before following her into the room. How was it that something as inane as hair soap could make her heartbeat rev up to double time, and make her palms sweat like a cold glass of lemonade on a hot day? It really had been too long.

Mel surveyed Georgia's reactions as she walked between the reptile tanks, silently peering into each one with a curious expression.

"Who's this one? What's his name?" she asked, pointing to the iguana.

"That's Sherbet. And she's a she," Mel said.

"Okay. Cute. And who's this?" Georgia pointed to the turtle.

"That's Pixie. Careful with that one. She almost took my finger off last time I fed her," she said. She followed Georgia to the gecko tank. "Lollipop is the brown-and-white one, and Gummy Bear is the yellow one." She waited for Georgia to approach the final tank, which housed a ball python snake named Slinky. Slinky was mellow and gentle, as well as nonvenomous, but Mel knew very few people who liked being in the presence of his sort. Time to see how much Georgia really wanted to volunteer at the shelter.

To Mel's surprise, Georgia scanned the tank and tapped quietly on the glass. "A snake," she said matter-of-factly.

"Slinky," said Mel. Georgia was full of surprises, she was starting to realize. "Most people don't want to go near him with a ten-foot pole."

"I lived outside the desert for a few years as a kid. Place was teeming with snakes," she said. "Okay, next stop?" Her sparkling hazel eyes ratcheted up Mel's heartbeat from double time to a full-on Ginger Rogers tap dance.

Next stop was the bunny room. Mel was doomed.

Georgia followed Mel through the animal shelter, meeting the different residents and trying to solicit the little information Mel seemed willing to share. Mel was curt with her explanations and checked her watch several times, and when Georgia asked her about her vet clinic and how long she'd been operating it, Mel made Georgia feel as though she'd asked for her blood type and password to her online banking account. Wasn't politeness supposed to be a thing in Canada?

She sensed that Mel had introduced her to Slinky the snake to get a rise out of her. It had taken everything in her to maintain her cool. The truth was, she hated snakes. As a child, when her parents were visiting professors at UC San Diego, she refused to go on hikes with them to Joshua Tree or Anza-Borrego because of what she'd read about the local residents of the parks, and on any trip to the zoo she'd skip the reptile pavilion. But she wasn't about to give Mel the satisfaction of seeing her as anything less than an animal lover in her first thirty minutes at the shelter. She needed this position.

Mel led her through the shelter's back door to the fenced-in outdoor space, where a series of pens with plywood roofs housed a variety of farm animals: a few goats, a potbellied pig, some ducks and a few others who must have been hiding in their homes.

"This is the outdoor crew," Mel said. "You'll mostly be feeding and watering them." She motioned for Georgia to follow her to the back pen. Damn it. The heels were definitely a mistake. Mel must have noticed her taking careful steps through the uneven gravel and sand, and extended her elbow for Georgia to grab on to. She paused for a moment, unsure about the sudden kind gesture, then placed her hand on Mel's forearm, grateful for the support and appreciative of the soft strength of it.

"She's not as cute as Slinky, but…" Mel pointed to a sandy-colored miniature horse with white hair, tucked in the back corner of her pen, with eyes so sad that Georgia instinctively wanted to take the animal into her arms. Snakes? No way. Horses? Now they were getting somewhere. "This is Taffy," Mel said, then whistled, and grabbed a carrot from the bucket outside of Taffy's pen. The little horse trotted over slowly, looking up at Georgia with curiosity.

"She's beautiful," Georgia breathed, then looked around at the collection of farm animals quietly going about their business in their pens. "Wouldn't a local farmer want to take them in?"

Mel passed Georgia the carrot, and she accepted. Their hands brushed together, and the warmth of Mel's skin felt like her California sunshine on the most perfect of days. Georgia clutched the carrot, then looked sideways at Mel to find the woman examining her, chocolate brown eyes pensive and deep, as though she was being tested. Georgia straightened her posture, and despite her heels digging into the gravel, took a few steps closer to Taffy's pen and extended the carrot to the horse, willing her to come closer.

"Some do," Mel said. "Depends on their backstory. Some of these were collected by the SPCA after a report of mistreatment. Others had to be given up by their owners once their farms were sold to developers. Lots of reasons why animals end up here," she said. "That one," Mel said, motioning to Taffy, "is infertile. Wouldn't sell at market. Not worth it for the breeder to house and feed her, so she got unloaded here." Mel's words carried a sharp sense of protectiveness.

"You poor thing," Georgia whispered, lightly running her hand over Taffy's soft head.

"She's gentle," Mel said. "Seamus is training her to be a therapy animal."

"I can see why."

"You're good with her," Mel said.

"You sound surprised." Georgia looked up to see if Mel's expression had changed, but it was still all business. She was a tough one to crack. But it wasn't Georgia's style to back down. "I was always jealous of the girls in my class who grew up on ranches," she said, remembering her peers who showed off their ribbons from horseback riding events during show-and-tell, or who spent their weekends riding the trails of the nearby canyons. In contrast, Georgia's weekends were spent doing reach-ahead math sessions with tutors and practicing the violin while her mother sat in the adjoining sitting room, tut-tutting every time Georgia made an error.

The idea of spending her day on a majestic horse, galloping beside a stream or across a palm oasis (high up and out of the reach of any snake, of course), was the stuff of many a daydream, and something she knew her mother and father would never go for.

"And you never went riding as a kid?" Mel asked.

"No," said Georgia. "My parents had my time pretty mapped out. But I plan on it, someday." She looked into Taffy's eyes, charmed by the animal's innocence and gentle nature. Maybe she could convince Seamus to keep her on Taffy duty.

Mel hadn't said a word, and Georgia looked to her side to see if she was still there. What had moments ago been an untrusting expression was now the slightest bit tender, as though she actually cared what Georgia had to say, and maybe, just maybe, was interested in hearing more.

Georgia paused for a moment, then opened her mouth, ready to continue, when Mel cleared her throat loudly, then checked her watch. "Well, gotta run," she said, looking away from Georgia, then starting back toward the shelter. She stopped, then turned back. "Need my help getting back?" she said, gesturing toward her heels, which were now covered in dirt.

"I'm okay," Georgia said. What had she done wrong? "I'm just going to spend a few more minutes out here looking around. You go ahead."

"Alright. I'm going to help Seamus out and lock up, so you can exit through the gate. See you around," Mel said, beelining back to the building.

"Wait," Georgia called, just before Mel could leave. She turned around, and Georgia took in her tall, lean body and the way her jeans hugged her hips perfectly. "You haven't told me which one is your favorite."

Mel raised her eyebrows, then chuckled. "I don't play favorites," she said. "You look long enough in

any of their eyes and you'll find something to love."
With that, she disappeared through the door, leaving
Georgia outside with her new charges.

She stood in the quiet of the shelter's outdoor space
and considered what Mel said, and the notion of having to look for something in someone to love. Was
that how it worked? Didn't love come easy, effortlessly, not like something you set out to do?

Not that she was looking to Mel Carter as the authority on all things love. The woman didn't exactly
have warm and fuzzy written all over her.

But that intent, searching look in her eyes, quietly
observing, was leading Georgia to believe that there
was a lot more under the surface, and maybe something that she was keeping hidden from the world.
Georgia prided herself in her ability to read people.
To know when they were telling the truth, when they
were lying, when they were afraid. It was part of why
she was so good at her work. But with Mel? It was
challenging.

Now she was working with her. Would Mel ever
reveal anything about herself to her? The idea was
intriguing, and just a bit nerve-racking.

You're here for a few weeks. A month, tops, she
reminded herself. In that amount of time, how much
of someone could you really know?

Chapter Four

Georgia studied the menu at Rise and Grind, the coffee shop near the water at the end of Main Street, trying to decide between ordering a medium roast and taking a chance on the special of the day, a pumpkin chai latté.

It was Monday morning, her first official shift at the shelter, and she was a bit unsure about what to expect. Seamus had called an hour earlier to say that his back had gotten worse, so Mel would be there to welcome her and give her a list of things that needed to be done. She hadn't expected to see Mel again until later in the week and was uncharacteristically nervous at the idea of spending the day alone with her.

Well, at least the animals would be there. But they couldn't be counted on for the type of polite conversation that might ease any tension.

Something she'd learned over and over in her work: if you're dealing with a difficult client, or trying to negotiate with a challenging opponent, you can never go wrong with the kill 'em with kindness approach.

"Just the latté?" asked the barista.

"Actually, make that two," said Georgia. "And I'll take a couple of croissants."

There. She'd show up at the shelter with a peace offering, although she still wasn't entirely sure why the gesture was necessary. Regardless, it was good form. Friendly professionalism. And Georgia loved a good challenge.

The shelter was just a short way up the street from Rise and Grind, so Georgia decided to leave her car where it was parked and walk a few minutes, enjoying the fall sunshine that provided some warmth in the cool, still air. She'd opted for a more sensible shoe this time around, nude Chloé ballet flats, which she'd paired with faded jeans and a gauzy red blouse, her hair tied back in a loose ponytail.

She took a deep breath before entering the shelter, balancing the tray of hot beverages and baked goods in one hand as she opened the door to the entrance with the other. She found Mel behind the reception desk, the phone cradled between her shoulder and cheek as she jotted something down on a pad of paper.

"Take a deep breath, Mrs. Crandles. It likely looks worse than it is. We'll have a look," Mel said, eyeing Georgia up and down at the same time. Was she judging her outfit again? Had Georgia known she'd be handling orphaned animals during her enforced stress break, she might have packed differently. But here she was.

Mel hung up, and Georgia watched while she extracted a file folder from behind the desk. "I'm glad you're here," she said, to Georgia's surprise. "I'm going to need your help in a few minutes."

"That's...why I'm here," Georgia said, placing the tray down on the counter and offering Mel her best winning smile. "Thought you might like a latté," she said. She pulled a cup from the tray and pushed it across the counter in Mel's direction. "I brought croissants too."

"Thanks. I don't drink caffeine, though," Mel said. Had Mel even heard of manners? She wasn't going to make this easy for her, was she? "But I'll take a croissant. Thanks." Mel cleared her throat, then flipped through the file folder she'd pulled. "That was Mrs. Crandles calling from her car. She's on her way over. She and her husband adopted Rocky a couple of weeks ago," she said, passing Mel a photo from the file. "She's concerned with what sounds like an abscess on the scar from the surgery he had before he left here. She's bringing him by so I can have a look."

"Okay, what can I do?" Georgia asked, surveying the picture of a little brown beagle. "Help hold him down while you examine him or something?" Mel smiled a half smile, and Georgia sensed a crack. "Distract him with an abandoned artisanal latté?"

"I can handle Rocky. I need you to hold down Mrs. Crandles."

"I am *all over* that," Georgia said. "Difficult people are my specialty."

"Oh yeah?" Mel said, cocking her head. "You a high school teacher or something? Prison warden?"

"Public relations," Georgia said, and took a sip of her drink. "Brand reputation and issues response."

"So, what does that mean? You cover for people who do bad things?"

"I prefer the term 'highlight the good.' I was premed at one point, actually."

Mel raised her eyebrows. Obviously she didn't see Georgia as the type. "Hmm," she said. "Doesn't explain why you're taking a sudden interest in animal rescue."

"What, a person can't be more than one thing?"

"That's not what I meant. You can't blame me for wondering why, when you've come all the way out here to settle your aunt's estate, you've made the decision to take on a whole other job."

"Nothing wrong with giving back now and then." Mel was onto her. Georgia straightened her shoulders, weighing whether or not she should disclose her motivation for volunteering. The idea of it made her feel uncharacteristically vulnerable. Mel had given no indication that she'd seen Georgia's video online, unlike half of the rest of the planet, and Georgia hadn't found Mel on any social media sites during her internet search, so chances were that she had no idea why the volunteer hours were part of Georgia's own PR strategy. Something told her that for whatever reason, Mel already had an unfavorable impression of her. No reason to make it any worse before it was necessary.

"Alright," Mel said, and looked up at her. "Thanks, by the way. My uncle runs himself ragged at this place. He loves it, but I worry about him sometimes." There it was again. Mel could be a prickly pear one minute, then say something that suggested her heart was not in fact made of stone the next.

Georgia was about to respond when the shelter's door flew open, and a silver-haired woman with frantic wide eyes entered, cradling a dog swaddled in a baby blue fleece blanket. "Dr. Carter," she said. "Thank you for seeing us right away." She approached Mel with her arms outstretched, and Mel accepted the bundle. "I'm so worried about our Rocky."

"Why don't I take Rocky back and have a look?" Mel said, peering down at the animal. "You can stay out here with Georgia, our new volunteer."

"I'll come with you," Mrs. Crandles said, almost knocking Georgia over to get to the back room. Mel shot Georgia a look.

"Actually, Mrs. Crandles," Georgia said. "Why don't you have a seat here for a few minutes? I'll get you a coffee. And," she said, pulling the latest *People* magazine out of her purse, "you can take a few minutes to get caught up on some gossip. Ben and J-Lo again, right? Who would have thought?"

Mrs. Crandles looked at Rocky, then back again at Georgia, and accepted the magazine without looking at it. "We won't be long," Mel assured the woman. "Make yourself comfortable. I'll call you back in a few minutes."

"Well, okay," Mrs. Crandles said, her voice laced with uncertainty.

Georgia turned toward the counter and winked at Mel, who mouthed "thanks," then disappeared into the back with Rocky, leaving Georgia with a very anxious Mrs. Crandles, who was looking out the window and twisting the magazine in her hands. If Georgia knew one thing about stressful situations, it was the power of distraction.

"Now, Mrs. Crandles. I happen to have a delicious latté here with your name on it. And a fresh croissant. How does that sound? Let's have a seat."

Within minutes, Georgia had Mrs. Crandles sipping her coffee and deep in conversation about the latest season of *The Bachelor*. Georgia was enjoying speaking with the woman, after so many days spent alone with little to no social interaction other than with Paulina. Not that she'd ever doubted it, but if she needed any confirmation that she was an extrovert, the last week had confirmed it.

Mrs. Crandles put her latté down and craned her neck to see what was going on in the back room. "I'd just never forgive myself if something happened to Rocky," she said, tearing up slightly.

"Well, you made the right choice bringing him here," Georgia said. "And he's in good hands." She had no knowledge of Mel's skills as a veterinarian, but she found herself making the claim with real confidence—not the type she sometimes had to put on when making a comment to the media or in a negotiation. There was something about Mel Carter that Georgia trusted. She was hard to read, to be sure, but some things you just felt.

Mel Carter made Georgia feel many other things too. But she was at work, and damn it if she wasn't a consummate pro. That's how Mel would see her.

From the examination room, Mel smiled to herself as she listened to Georgia regaling Mrs. Crandles with stories from backstage on a movie shoot with some celebrity Mel had never heard of. Mrs. Crandles had momentarily forgotten why she was there, and Mel was grateful. It was hard enough working with animals to begin with without an anxious pet owner breathing down her neck. Animals didn't always understand you were trying to help them, not like humans who could rationalize that a little discomfort or pain was sometimes necessary to achieve a better outcome.

Mel was also trying to make sense of the shiver

running down her spine and radiating through all four limbs, which had been activated with Georgia's conspiratorial wink and smile only moments ago in the reception area. She radiated a confidence that not only assured Mel she would keep Mrs. Crandles off her back while she did her work, but that was also undeniably sexy.

Mel listened to Georgia laughing, remembering the way she threw her head back when Franny had jumped up on her on the road outside of her place, and how much her smile showed in her eyes.

Oh, man. She was losing it.

She shook her head as she examined the small, docile puppy on the examination table. Rocky had a tiny abscess on his surgery scar that would disappear in a few days with a course of antibiotics. It was slightly inflamed, likely from Rocky licking it, but it was nothing to worry about. He'd just have to wear a cone until it healed. While it was clear that Mrs. Crandles had overreacted, Mel would never fault her patients' owners for caring about their pets. Especially ones like Rocky, who had been through a lot, and who Mel was thrilled to see had found a safe and caring, if slightly overbearing, home.

She took a moment to gather herself before she brought Rocky back out to the reception area. What was she going to do with Georgia after Mrs. Crandles left? She hadn't expected to be spending the morning training a new volunteer. A volunteer who filled the room with the type of energy that she'd been working to avoid for so long.

"What do you think, Rocky? Am I going off the deep end here?" Mel said aloud, scratching the dog behind his ears, much to Rocky's delight. She gave Rocky a treat from a jar on the counter, loving how gratefully the dog gobbled it up—a deliberate distraction while Mel fastened the plastic cone around his neck. "Come on. Let's get you on your way."

She deposited Rocky on the ground, clipped on his leash and allowed him to lead the way back to the reception area.

"My baby!" Mrs. Crandles said, jumping out of her chair, her hands clasped across her chest. Mel let go of the leash and let Rocky run over to his owner, pleased to see how quickly they'd formed a bond since his adoption.

She glanced up at Georgia, who was grinning with those perfect, glossy pink lips from ear to ear. Georgia looked over at her, catching her eye. Mel's stomach bottomed out and she instinctively wanted to flee to the back room.

After she'd sent Mrs. Crandles and Rocky on their way, cone intact and with instructions for administering the course of antibiotics, she was alone again with Georgia, who was looking at her expectantly, awaiting instructions.

"Ah, let's see," Mel said, trying to think of something simple she could set Georgia up to do before

heading back to her clinic, where an afternoon of appointments awaited her. "How long are you here for
again?"

"Today?" Georgia said. Some silky strands of hair
had come loose from her ponytail, framing her face
perfectly. She wasn't making it any easier on Mel.
"I told Seamus I'd come for four hours. I have a real
estate agent coming to Nina's this afternoon."

"Alright," Mel said. "How do you feel about spending some time with the bunnies? They just need some
playtime. Socialization." Any other task would require training, and Mel could probably get the feeding
and cleaning of the other cages and pens done in half
the time it would take to show Georgia what to do.

"Um, that's like asking someone how they feel
about freshly baked chocolate chip cookies."

"They're not always as cute as you think. But don't
worry, we'll get you working with Slinky next time
you're here."

Georgia laughed. "Who said I was afraid of snakes?"

"Last time you were here? You played it cool. But
I saw the terror in your eyes."

"Just show me the bunnies," Georgia said, taking
a step closer, a playful look challenging Mel to keep
teasing her. "Socializing is one of my best skills."

Mel tried to keep from smiling. Of course it was.
A woman as stunning and charming as Georgia?
She was the type who walked into a room, lit it up
and within moments had people coming out of the

woodwork to be by her side, to bask in that radiant light. Mel was heating up as if that light was a sunbeam directed right at her.

"Alright then," Mel said. "After you."

She spent a few minutes showing Georgia some techniques for working with the bunnies, like using blueberries to get them to sit in her lap, or to touch their noses to a ball. When she'd had enough of that, she should clean the litter boxes. Mel noted that Georgia was wearing more appropriate attire than her initial visit, but she still managed to make jeans and a blouse look like a million bucks.

"There are aprons behind the door and gloves on the counter over there," Mel said as she watched Georgia on the floor, patting the bunnies. It was quite the sight, and for a moment, counter to her instincts, she felt compelled to stay around a little longer.

"This is fun," Georgia said, cupping a little white bunny in her hands. "What's your name?"

"That's Mr. Dimiglio," Mel said.

Georgia's face lit up with amusement. "Who names the animals here?"

"Some come to us with names. Otherwise, the students at the local school that come here now and then for field trips usually have naming rights. Some of them are weird. But the kids seem to love it."

"Well, okay, Mr. Dimiglio," Georgia cooed, giving the bunny a gentle kiss on his head. "Not sure that's the name I would have chosen for you, but you're still cute."

Was it weird that Mel was jealous of a bunny? Yes. It was weird. Time to go. "Alright, well, I'd better head out," Mel said, looking at her watch. How had the time passed so quickly? She enjoyed working with her uncle, but she'd be lying if she said that the shelter wasn't all of a sudden a much more exciting place to be. "Hope you don't mind locking up. The door uses a digital keypad. What's your number? I'll text you the code."

Mel saw what she thought was a flash of disappointment in Georgia's eyes. *Don't be stupid*, she thought. She'd spent the morning being a less than friendly host. If anything, Georgia was probably glad Mel was leaving.

"My first day, and I'm already getting the keys to the kingdom?" Georgia asked. "Wow, you must really trust me."

I really don't. Or maybe I just don't trust myself. That's why I need to get the heck out of here, Mel thought. "Small town, remember?" she said. "Not sure we even need to lock the door, anyway. Maybe it's more to keep these animals from staging an escape."

"I don't know why they'd want to leave. It's a pretty great place here." Georgia smiled, and Mel's heart swelled at the compliment.

Georgia recited her number, and Mel sent her the code and gave a few last instructions for closing up.

"And just call if you need anything," she said, turning to leave.

"Okay, 10-4," said Georgia.

Mel took one more quick look back before leaving the room, only to see Georgia nuzzle Mr. Dimiglio to her nose, then slide her phone out of her pocket to take a selfie of her with the bunny. Mel shook her head. The impromptu photo shoot aside, she actually did trust leaving Georgia at the shelter to care for the animals. It was an unfounded trust, to be sure, and maybe it was just the confidence and competence she radiated, but Mel was surprised by the calm she felt leaving things in Georgia's hands.

Watch that, she reminded herself, gathering her things at the front reception. She'd trusted too easily once before. *And look how that turned out.*

"Looks good in here, overall," Hayley Chapman said, surveying Nina's cottage, iPad in hand. The Realtor typed out a few notes and took some pictures of the different rooms, making suggestions for things to do before putting the cottage on the market. She stopped in the living room, and Georgia waited for her to make a comment about the amazing view.

"Now that—" Hayley said, wriggling her nose and pointing to the couch "—has to go before we even think about showings."

Days ago, Georgia would have agreed wholeheartedly. But, after several days of curling up on the corduroy couch in front of the fireplace, luxuriating in the worn-in, pillowy softness? She had to mask that she was slightly offended at the criticism of her new favorite piece of furniture. Maybe she'd bring it back to LA. She smiled to herself, thinking of the newly beloved eyesore among the clean modern lines and all-beige furniture in her place. *Maybe not.*

"The market's great right now. Not to put too much pressure on, but I'd say we have a week, maybe two, before the peak starts to dip. If you want to get top dollar for this place, I'd suggest getting on it before the snow comes."

Georgia nodded. Trying to sell the place for as much as possible would allow her to execute the next phase in her return-to-form agenda. Her plan was to take the proceeds and make a very generous (and very public) donation to Aurelia Martin's charity, a trust for sustainable forestry. She didn't need the money, and besides, Nina had always been very generous and would have loved to see her money go to a good cause. It was a win-win if Georgia had ever seen one. And the timing was just right.

"I'll have everything ready for you to take pictures tomorrow," Georgia said. She had day shifts scheduled at the shelter for the rest of the week, so she would take the evening to pack away any personal items and rearrange the furniture and decor as per Hayley's suggestions.

"Good of you to do this for your aunt," Hayley said.

"We were close," said Georgia. "Did you know her?"

Hayley nodded. "Everyone knew Nanny. She was never my teacher but I always saw her cruising around on her bike. She was in good shape. I was surprised to hear that she'd passed."

Georgia paused. "Ovarian cancer," she said quietly. It really wasn't fair. Nina had done things right. Exercised, ate well, spent time in nature and had a busy job, but one Georgia knew had brought her fulfillment.

And life had still dealt her a raw hand.

"Listen," Hayley said. "I know you'll be busy over the next while. But if you ever need a break and want to go out for a drink or something, let me know."

Georgia smiled gratefully. *Small towns.* "That's really nice of you," she said. "But between this and helping out at the animal shelter—"

"At the shelter?" Hayley said. "Huh. You must know Mel."

At the mention of Mel's name, Georgia felt her pulse speed up. "Yeah, we've met," she said, trying to act cool. "Her uncle hurt his back, so I think she's taking over a bit. And I'm helping out while I'm here. How do you know her?"

For a brief moment, Georgia was prepared for Hayley to say that she more than knew Mel, that maybe they were in a relationship. Hayley was a natural beauty—long, dark wavy hair, deep blue eyes and a perfect olive complexion. She could see Hayley being Mel's type. Based on the zero information she had about Mel's type.

"She and my sister used to be really close," Hayley said. "Grade school, high school, university…" Georgia noted her hesitancy as she trailed off. She didn't press, hoping Hayley would offer more. *Used to be? What did that mean?* "I thought she was so cool when I was growing up," she continued. "My friends always wanted to come over, on the off chance that she'd be there." She laughed. "Anyway. Well, sounds like you'll be busy. But the offer still stands if you change your mind. There's an open mic at The Hidden Oar Tavern tonight that's kind of fun. Depending on who's playing, of course."

"Thanks," Georgia said. It didn't seem as though Hayley recognized her either. Either the entire population of Sunset County lived under a rock, or they were just living up to the small-town reputation for politeness. Whatever it was, Georgia appreciated it.

She saw Hayley out, then spent the next two hours organizing things into boxes: most items destined for donations, and some in a small box that she would keep, to remember her aunt. A few framed photos of the two of them, from a trip to Disneyland and from Georgia's high school graduation. Her aunt's handwritten recipe book. The pair of sapphire earrings she'd given Nina for her fiftieth birthday. A set of diaries that she couldn't bring herself to read, but that she didn't want falling into any other hands, out of respect for Nina's privacy.

Georgia had never kept a diary. Who would ever record all their innermost secrets for someone else to come across? Not her.

She thought about what she'd write if she were to make a diary entry of that day. The fact that she was developing a full-blown crush on Dr. Mel Carter? She laughed to herself. A crush? What a teenager. But come on. Mel was objectively *hot*. And kind of unapproachable, that hard-to-get unavailable quality that was so annoyingly attractive. What was the evolutionary advantage of *that*? She shook her head, the same way she did every time she caught herself thinking like her scientist parents.

And then there was the fact that Mel took care of *kittens* for a living. Talk about a walking PR strategy for hookups.

After two hours of sorting through papers, folding clothes and moving furniture, Georgia flopped back on the couch, lacking the energy to start a fire. She was tired—physically, but also emotionally. While she was approaching the task with the same matter-of-factness that she did any work, more than once throughout the evening she'd choked up, thinking of her aunt, overwhelmed with the knowledge that she'd lost her closest family member and friend.

The sun had just dipped behind the trees on the other side of the lake, the sky glowing an orangey pink and making dark silhouettes out of the trees surrounding the water. If she weren't so exhausted, it would be a beautiful evening for a walk.

It was also a beautiful evening for pepperoni pizza.

Georgia picked up her phone to search for the number of a local pizza place and noticed on her screen that she'd missed a call.

Her stomach almost bottomed out when she saw the caller ID. *Mario Kimpton.* Senior Partner at Herstein PR Agency, the man responsible for Georgia's hiring and the very same man responsible for Georgia being forced to take a break from her job.

Had he seen the strategic pic she'd posted on her Instagram with her and the bunny, with a caption that made it very clear she was being a model citizen during her time away from work?

She tapped in her passcode and put her voicemail on speaker, heart pounding in her chest as she awaited what felt like a verdict in a criminal trial.

"Georgia." Mario's deep, gruff voice came through the phone. "Speaking on behalf of all of us here when I say we hope you're doing okay. I'm sending along some forms from HR. Just some formalities about your leave. Thought I'd give you a heads-up in case you weren't checking your email. Take care."

Her heart pounded in her chest as she hung up the phone and lay back on the couch, trying to steady her breathing. It wasn't bad news. But it wasn't good news either.

Suddenly she was filled with nervous energy, and no longer saw herself lying on the couch all night eating pizza.

She picked up her phone and dialed Hayley's number. Sure, she was here to take care of some business. But that didn't mean she couldn't have a bit of fun at the same time, did it?

Chapter Five

Mel wiped a layer of ice shavings off the blade of her skate with her sock, her fingers and toes burning with the sudden return of blood to her extremities. As she shed her hockey equipment one piece at a time, stowing everything away in her bag, she listened to her teammates' banter, good-natured ribbing and analysis of who played the best that game.

It was just Monday night house league hockey with a group of women well past their prime, looking to get out of the house and relive the glory of their younger days, but Mel loved the game and appreciated the chance to work up a sweat. This game, however, she'd been dreading.

The game itself was fine—she'd even managed to

put away two goals. It was what came after the game that she really wasn't looking forward to.

It wasn't that she didn't like the girls on the team, she just had no interest in the social aspect of playing a team sport—the regular post-game drinks and nachos. She kept a friendly distance from her teammates, played her game and engaged in the locker room, but only joined in on the visit to the pub once a year. It was a tradition that each player bought the first round once a season, and tonight was her night.

It would be fine. She'd go, make some mindless small talk, eat a few wings, then pick up the tab and get back to her place before the god-awful open mic started. Make some dinner, check in on her uncle Seamus and aunt Connie, maybe call her parents down in Florida, watch the news then get to bed. Some people might call her antisocial, but her lifestyle suited her.

Ever since Lauren's betrayal, she mostly kept to herself. She was a grown woman with no need for "buddies." If she wanted to socialize, she'd go over to her sister's place and spend time with Andie and the boys.

"Big night, ladies!" exclaimed Erin Dawes, the team goalie and the most likely to be last to leave the pub that night. "Carter's gracing us with her presence!"

A few scattered hoots and hollers from the rest of the team confirmed that Mel was not unwelcome, but that her presence wasn't necessarily going to be the highlight of the night.

Half an hour later, Mel was perched on a pub stool at The Hidden Oar, which was sandwiched on the north side of Main Street in between the bookshop and the radio station, watching one of her teammates make an idiot of herself in an unsuccessful and embarrassing attempt to hit on their server.

"Sorry about her," Mel said to the young guy taking their orders, who seemed intimidated by the table of raucous women. "She's a lightweight."

Mel's comment caused an eruption among the rest of the team, and Kassie elbowed her in the ribs playfully. "You gotta come out more often!" she said.

"Maybe I should." Mel knew very well that the next time she'd be joining the group, it would be the next time she was in charge of buying a round.

Truth was, hanging out with her teammates after the game really wasn't all that bad. And for the most part, the conversation stuck to fairly surface topics like sports, local news or upcoming travel plans, but every now and then someone asked a question or made a comment that bordered on personal, something involving a relationship or the like. That's when Mel started to check her watch, dreading the moment someone asked something about her and her life. Hopefully, they knew enough not to wade into that territory.

"Alright, cheers, ladies!" Erin exclaimed, and Mel calculated that she must have been on her fourth helping from the pitchers on the table, judging from the slight redness in her cheeks and her jubilant raise of her glass, which sloshed a bit of beer down her forearm.

Just as Mel raised her glass for the obligatory cheers, she noticed the pub's door swing open, and a familiar face entered the room, searching the crowd for whoever it was she was there to meet.

Mel hadn't seen Hayley Chapman in person in over two years, but was used to seeing her on For Sale signs around town. She was the spitting image of her sister, both of them tall with dark hair and crystal blue eyes and the same quick smile, the one Mel had elicited so many times in Lauren joking around while they were growing up.

Mel had always liked Hayley. She probably still would have liked her, if it wasn't for the company she kept. Not that people could choose their families.

Mel looked away, trying to avoid catching Hayley's eye, but allowed herself to glance over when the door opened again. Whoever had just entered was the person Hayley had been looking for. Mel tried to turn her attention back to her tablemates, but when she glanced over again she was surprised to see none other than Georgia O'Neill enter the pub. Tonight, Georgia's hair was loose around her shoulders, and she wore a tight, low-cut top showing just enough skin to make Mel shift in her seat.

What was Georgia doing there with Hayley? Pretending to listen to the woman across from her provide her analysis on the top contenders for the Super Bowl, Mel watched out of the corner of her eye as Hayley and Georgia took a seat only three booths over, close enough that Mel would probably catch snippets of their conversation if she listened closely enough. Hayley must be working with Georgia on the sale, she realized.

It was time to pay the bill and get out of there.

"Earth to Carter," Erin was saying, waving a hand in her face.

"Sorry," Mel said, clearing her throat. "Just thought I saw someone I knew."

Erin turned and looked in the direction Mel had been focusing. "Hey, isn't that—" Erin nudged Kassie, and pointed toward Georgia and Hayley. Mel motioned to the server to bring the check. She was only supposed to buy the first round, but she'd cover the entire tab to get out of there as quickly as possible. She fished for her wallet in her coat pocket, trying to figure out how she'd get out of the pub without passing Georgia and Hayley's table. There was a back exit, wasn't there?

"That's totally her!" Erin said, now finished with yet another pint. Mel was surprised she could see five feet in front of her. "She's—" She paused, searching.

"From the real estate billboards. Yeah," Mel said. The server passed her the bill and she handed him her credit card without looking.

"Nah, not her. The light-haired one. That's the one from the video!"

"It totally is," said Kassie. "But what's she doing here? Isn't she like, famous or something?"

They must have been mistaken. Too much beer. Mel watched as Kassie searched something on her phone, then flashed the screen to the rest of the table. "It's her! That video was all over social media!"

Mel sat back in her seat, trying not to react as her teammates discussed whatever video they were referring to in low voices, craning their necks to get a better glimpse. How did they know Georgia? What video were they talking about? Mel was curious, but she was even more mortified by the idea of Georgia seeing her teammates gossiping about her.

At this point, Mel was almost willing to leave her credit card behind. She had to escape.

"Oh no, she's coming over," Kassie said, a hint of glee and panic in her voice. "Play it cool."

"Don't you know it's impolite to stare?" Mel heard Georgia's unmistakable, self-assured voice directly over her shoulder. It was Mel's fault for drawing Erin's attention to Georgia. If she could just melt into the floor, she would.

"We're sorry," Kassie said, grinning sheepishly. "We just—we just recognized you, and our friend here had never heard of you, so…"

Mel felt Georgia's eyes burning a hole in the back of her head. She turned around to find Georgia standing right over her shoulder. When she realized it was Mel at the table, Georgia's expression changed from bemused to…what was it? Hurt? Embarrassed? Betrayed? A mix of all three? Whatever it was, Mel's stomach lurched at the sight of it and she knew she had to do damage control.

"Georgia, hey," Mel said.

"Mel?"

An extended awkward pause filled the air while Mel's teammates tried to make sense of how she knew Georgia O'Neill, and Mel tried to figure out how to navigate the situation. She had to say something, but couldn't find the words.

"Alright, well, I'll let you all get back to having fun." Georgia spun around and walked back to her table, leaving all Mel's teammates staring at her, waiting for an explanation.

"Carter," Kassie finally said. "We've always known you're mysterious, but—"

She mumbled something about Georgia volunteering at the shelter while she scooped up her credit card from the table, and all but raced out the door.

In the back alley behind the pub where her car was parked, Mel paused to collect herself, replaying what had just happened inside. She felt like an idiot for running out like that, but what was she supposed to do? Introduce Georgia, who was clearly caught off guard and embarrassed about whatever video her teammates were going on about, to a team of buzzed hockey players? Or walk Georgia back to her table and make idle chitchat with her and Hayley, who she hadn't spoken to since her sister destroyed their friendship?

No. She'd made the right decision by leaving.

So why did it feel so wrong?

"Sorry," Georgia said, sliding into her seat.

"You okay? What happened?" Hayley asked, her blue eyes full of concern.

"Ugh. Why is it that women in a group revert to immature, gossipy teenagers?" Georgia said, taking a long sip of her chardonnay. "I just asked them to stop staring over here."

"Well," said Hayley. "Bronzed beauty? Never been seen around here? Can't say I'm surprised."

"Anyway," Georgia said, eager to change the subject.

"You know," Hayley said, hesitantly, "people will forget about that video in no time."

"Aha. I wondered if you'd seen it."

Hayley gave her a tight smile. "Well. I will admit that I'm always curious about my clients. And your aunt Nina always spoke about you. So when I learned I'd be working with you on the sale, I looked you up, and…"

"And you were treated to a clip of my sensational meltdown," Georgia said, the all-too-familiar wave of embarrassment she'd been swimming in over the past couple of weeks washing over her. Coming out with Hayley tonight was a mistake.

"Listen. Like I said, it'll blow over. And I have to say you looked incredible in that gold dress. What was that, Armani?"

"Saint Laurent," Georgia said. If there was an upside to the entire thing, that was the truth. She'd felt terrible that night, all frayed nerves and exhaustion, but her makeup artist had erased the bags under her eyes, and the sleek chignon her hairstylist had woven gave her the air of someone much more pulled together than she felt. She looked great in the mirror. And in the video too, at least from the neck down, if you discounted the look of pure rage on her face as she hurled both expletives and an opulent Bordeaux.

"Well, you looked fab. And we all have our moments."

"Yeah. Most of them don't get broadcast to the entire world, though."

Hayley smiled sympathetically. "How about another round? On me," she said. "We're more than our mistakes."

Despite the sliver of disappointment Georgia felt that she wasn't going to be maintaining her anonymity in Sunset County, she got the sense that Hayley really didn't care.

"Amen to that," Georgia said, though when it came to herself, she disagreed very much with the idea.

One more drink would be good. The idea of going

back to Nina's alone wasn't too appealing to her, and some more time at the pub and the distraction of conversation might take the edge off the fact that Mel had barely acknowledged her moments ago. After their interaction that morning, she'd started to see a crack in Mel's tough exterior, a kindness that gave her the sense they might enjoy working together over the coming days. Now Georgia realized she was wrong. Whatever. She'd be professional, put in some hours and get a few more good selfies for her social media while she was at it. At least now Mel might understand what Georgia was doing at the shelter.

Georgia took a quick look back at the table of women, whose increasing volume and exuberant gesturing indicated they'd likely had more than two drinks. She also noticed that Mel had left.

"Hey, you mentioned that your sister and Mel Carter used to be friends?" Georgia asked, once again trying not to appear overly interested.

Hayley's expression changed. She took a deep breath and sighed. "Yeah. They haven't spoken in a while."

Georgia waited a moment, a classic interviewing technique for trying to solicit more information from someone. People had the tendency to jump in before the subject had fully shared a thought or had some time to think.

She waited until the moment just before it got awkward and realized Hayley might not be about to share any more. "Huh," Georgia said. "What does your sister do?"

"Lauren's a forest ranger. Lives two towns over. The stereotype of a screw-up older sister," Hayley said, rolling her eyes. "We're all waiting for her to grow up. A great person but has some maturing to do."

Why she cared so much about Mel's relationship with her former best friend, Georgia didn't know, but maybe it was the idea that someone had been really close to Mel, who seemed so unknowable and impenetrable.

The table of women erupted in laughter. "Speaking of immature," Hayley said, rolling her eyes again. "This is why I have no friends. No options around here. Please take me back to LA with you."

"Ha," Georgia said. "I'm afraid people in LA have their own issues."

"Well, who needs 'em?" Hayley said, holding up her wine goblet.

Georgia clinked her glass against Hayley's. "Who needs 'em."

"Who needs 'em, indeed," Georgia muttered an hour later, as she pulled her pajama top over her head, then moved into the bathroom to wash off her makeup. The whole cab ride home, she'd pondered the question, a question she asked herself every now and then, on nights like this when she was returning home to an empty place.

Generally, she liked the solitude and independence that came with living alone. Everything the way you wanted it. Coming and going as you pleased. No one infringing on your side of the bed and interfering with precious sleep hours, or leaving globs of toothpaste in the sink. Her job was inherently social, so she never really felt lonely, but there were times when she felt a tinge of longing for a light to be on inside when she arrived home, or someone there to greet her and listen to her talk about her day.

Tonight was one of those nights.

But, she reminded herself, Nina had fared okay without a partner. Or had she? She always seemed to be completely happy on her own and never spoke of having or wanting romance in her life.

And really, who had time to date? Georgia's hectic work schedule left her about ninety minutes to herself each day, forty-five of which were required for exercise and the other to make dinner and catch a few minutes of news or a scene or two from whatever show she was onto at the time. The rare weekends she wasn't at an event were for catching up on emails, a trip to the spa, and maybe dinner and drinks with Paulina if she had the energy.

The thing was, a question continued to run through her head. *Who needs 'em?* Maybe *she* did. And maybe it was the wine, but every thought of her hand in hand with someone, smiling and laughing and sharing dreams about the future, included Mel Carter, her deep brown eyes holding hers, sitting across from her at a candlelit restaurant; lighting a fire in Nina's living room and returning to the couch with a glass of wine; walking through the woods together with Franny bounding through the trees ahead of them. Opening the door and welcoming her home. Taking her in her strong arms and telling her that everything was going to be okay. Maybe she needed that.

Georgia shook her head and made a mental note to order food the next time she was presented with two nine-ounce glasses of cheap house wine.

Strange, dreamy and far-fetched thoughts about Mel Carter aside, the idea of cramming a dating life into her jam-packed schedule seemed all but impossible. Maybe once she was more established in her career, and once she'd smoothed things over. Then she could take her foot off the gas a bit. But in the meantime, there was no time for distraction.

Her plan was to work in this new role for a few years, and then attain her ultimate goal: Chief Client Officer. The top dog at the company, aside from Mario, of course. Viola Alves was close to retirement, and there would be fierce competition for her job. Georgia knew that to contend for her position, not only did she have to hit it out of the park in her new role, but she also had to show complete dedication to the company, which meant attending every event possible, nonstop networking and accessing as much face time with Mario, Viola and the other executive, Liz, as possible.

If, in fact, she still had a job.

Pajamas on, face cleansed and not yet tired enough to go to sleep, Georgia slumped into her favorite spot on the corduroy couch (which she'd vetoed for removal) and picked up her phone. She dialed her voicemail and replayed the message from Mario Kimpton that had given her such hope only hours ago, listening intently for any signs in his voice that the news would be anything but positive. *We hope you're doing okay.* Who was *we*? Was it just a pleasantry? Something to placate her until they pulled the rug out from under her? And then there was the fact that they were sending her official HR forms. Was that the first legal step in terminating an employee? *Termination?* Was she going off the deep end?

Had she gone off the deep end?

Tucked away in the woods in the middle of nowhere, about to get to bed in time to wake up for hours of feeding bunnies and an assortment of unwanted reptiles?

This is temporary, she reminded herself. *And when I'm back, I'll be better than ever.*

The little pony whinnied when Mel approached her pen, bag of feed in hand. The morning was crisp and cool, and Mel's breath was visible in the air, the early sunlight casting long shadows across the shelter's exterior pens.

"C'mere, Taffy," she called, then whistled. "Good girl," she said, removing her leather work glove to stroke the side of Taffy's face right under her eye as she nuzzled into Mel's hand.

For what seemed like the hundredth time that morning while she completed the outdoor chores, Mel glanced sideways at the back entrance to the shelter, waiting for Georgia to pop her head through and announce her presence. Now, at twenty minutes past the time she was due to begin her shift, Mel was starting to think she wasn't coming. And she wouldn't blame her. Not after the pathetic showing from her and her teammates the night before.

She had to apologize when Georgia arrived. Although apologizing would communicate that she cared about being on good terms with her, Mel felt the need to separate herself from the drunken Neanderthal behavior of her teammates. She was many things, but she was never disrespectful to people, and hated the idea of being seen as such.

"There you go," she said, as she filled Taffy's trough with alfalfa-mixed hay. She stood back and watched as Taffy sniffed her breakfast, then started to take small bites. While the backlog of appointments at her clinic was piling up now that she had to fill in for Seamus, moments like this, in the quiet peace of the morning, made the extra work worthwhile. Not to mention, working side by side with Georgia.

Maybe it would be for the best if Georgia didn't show. The nerves in the pit of her stomach, the ones that had been churning since the night before, might finally go away. And that sinking, unwelcome feeling she couldn't seem to put away since she'd met Georgia O'Neill, the one that told her the woman was something special, well, she could finally put that to bed.

Right on cue, and as though the universe had other, more complicated plans, the back door opened and Georgia stepped out, her caramel-colored tresses spilling out from under a light blue wool hat, coffee cup in hand. Mel noticed she hadn't brought her anything this time, but warmed at the thought of Georgia thinking about her the day before. Georgia waved and smiled, and at once, Mel's nerves were swirling in a tornado of attraction.

"Sorry I'm late," Georgia said, pulling the zipper of her down puffer jacket right up to her chin. She stopped in her tracks, taking a deep breath and surveying the surroundings. "What a gorgeous morning! And yeah, sorry, the lineup at Rise and Grind was out the door. But trust me, you don't want me uncaffeinated."

The truth was, Mel wanted her in any form. Caffeinated, uncaffeinated, tired, perky—whatever Georgia was bringing, Mel was taking.

Georgia approached where Mel was standing, and a sudden breeze carried the sweet scent of her perfume, her shampoo, whatever it was—her delicious scent—over to her, announcing her presence to every sense receptor in her body.

"No worries," Mel said. "I saved Slinky and friends for you."

Georgia smiled, and Mel marveled at how an already sunny yard could all of a sudden get that much brighter. She noticed that Georgia wasn't wearing very much makeup, unlike the other times she'd seen her. She was a total stunner, a natural beauty. "Very funny. But I think I made some real progress with the bunnies the other day. We've got some momentum going with their training, so..."

"Alright," Mel said, grinning despite herself. "You up for helping me for a few minutes out here first?" She didn't really need the help, but it might give her the opportunity to apologize for last evening. She cringed, remembering Georgia's face as it showed the slightest of crumples, the tiniest crack in her consistently confident presentation.

The same confidence that was causing Mel's body to hum from head to toe. Best to rip off the bandage. "Listen, uh, about last night—"

"Don't mention it," Georgia said, waving her off. "You think that was bad? Try reading a sample of the comments about my meltdown."

"Not sure what meltdown you mean," Mel said.

"But those women…they're idiots. And had a few too many. They're just girls I play hockey with. Not friends or anything." She'd already apologized—why was she feeling the need to overexplain?

"Well, I won't argue with that," Georgia said. "So, I take it you hadn't seen the video until last night?"

"Still haven't. Must have been some video, though." Mel had been tempted to see what all the fuss was about, but when she was weighing the idea of looking up Georgia's name online, instead of curiosity, all she felt was a nagging feeling of protectiveness toward Georgia and her privacy. Someone or something had obviously hurt her, and Mel refused to believe that she was capable of doing anything that warranted that level of public scrutiny. Georgia could share with her if she wanted. And if not, that was her decision.

"It was something. And I don't believe you," Georgia said, then paused. "Actually, maybe I do. I'm just surprised you haven't seen it already."

"I don't go online a lot," Mel said. "Seems like a waste of time to me. Maybe that's an unpopular opinion." Mel studied Georgia's face, gauging if she believed her, until she turned toward Taffy's pen, leaning over the gate and extending her hand until Taffy approached, sniffing her wrist. Mel watched as Georgia fawned over the pony, as though they were in their own little world together, until she turned back to Mel, that bright smile lighting up her eyes.

"It's an opinion that would probably put my industry out of business if it caught on," Georgia said. "You're not wrong, though."

"Well, in any event, I wanted to apologize. Whatever happened, it's your business. And you don't deserve a bunch of drunken rec league hockey players ruining your night out." There. She'd said it. Accepting the apology would be up to Georgia, but no one could say Mel hadn't done the right thing. But the idea that Georgia had done something bad enough that people recognized her in public? Maybe she shouldn't have given her the security code.

But then. Then there was the natural and warm way she connected with Taffy. Her gentle approach with the bunnies. How she'd jumped to help Seamus when he hurt his back and held his hand until he'd assured her he was okay. It didn't add up.

"It didn't ruin my night. I was just—" She paused. "I was just surprised to see you."

Mel wasn't sure how to take that, so she just waited.

"Shall we get to work?" Georgia asked, pulling off her hat, running her fingers through her glossy hair, then settling it back on her head.

Who knew that pulling on a wool hat could be so incredibly sexy? Mel tried to focus on what she was saying, and not what it would feel like to have her own fingers trailing through Georgia's hair, then down the smooth skin of her neck.

"After you," Mel said. She motioned toward the back door. "I have a special project for you today."

"I'm intrigued!" said Georgia. "Does it involve spiders? I don't do spiders."

"No spiders," Mel said. "Although we have had a tarantula in the past."

"Why anyone would ever want that as a pet is beyond me. Isn't the point to have something soft and cuddly to snuggle up with? Like Franny—there's a pet I can get behind."

Mel smiled as she opened the door for Georgia, wondering at the same time if she could push back her late morning appointments at the clinic. With Georgia's late arrival, she'd only have an hour with her and it just didn't seem like enough. Then again, her schedule might be doing her a real favor. Every extra minute with Georgia was a slippery slope to a place where Mel was afraid to go.

For a moment, she thought back to the early days with Breanne, and the all-encompassing fixation of a new relationship. They'd spent every waking moment together, parting ways only to attend their classes and grab the odd coffee or drinks with friends, always finding excuses to leave early and spend entire nights in each other's arms, all wrapped up in the magnetic attraction and mutual adoration.

Mel had lost herself then, and had paid the price twice over. And this intoxicating infatuation that was developing—she knew full well where this could lead.

"So, what's the special project?" Georgia said. "Day

two, and I'm already being promoted to top-level duties?"

"Ha," Mel said. "Kind of, I guess. More like essential services." She motioned toward the office, where a stack of paperwork sat awaiting filing. "It's not glamorous, but we need to keep track of each animal's history: how they ended up here, any required treatment and then paperwork of the adoption trail. You can feel free to look at a few completed files to see how Seamus likes everything organized. If you're able to make any progress on that pile, that would be really helpful."

"On it," Georgia said, picking up some loose papers from the top of the stack and leafing through them.

"Just…be prepared. Remember that some of these animals came to us in pretty rough shape." Mel stood in the doorway and observed as Georgia shuffled through the documentation, and held her breath as she picked up another file, the one she knew contained a photo of a rescue dog who had been locked in its owner's basement for weeks without food, and who was skin and bones by the time he arrived at the shelter.

Georgia looked up at Mel, tears glistening in her eyes. "How could anyone do something like this?" she asked, a waver in her voice. Mel immediately regretted assigning her the filing task without any preparation for what was contained in the files. Mel, unfortunately, had seen many similar images, had held those very animals in her arms and found it to be a challenging experience. Of course it would be upsetting for Georgia to see. What was she thinking?

"I'm sorry, maybe this isn't the best—"

"I can do it," Georgia said, wiping her eyes. "I just can't believe… Why would someone ever get a pet, just to treat it like that?"

"Lots of crummy people in this world," Mel said, swallowing hard and resisting the urge to pull Georgia into her arms, wipe the tears from her eyes and lay her head on her chest.

Wordlessly, Georgia walked the stack of papers over to the filing cabinet. "Do the current animals have folders too?" Georgia asked. "If I get through these, I'd like to see the folders in progress as well."

"There," Mel said, pointing to another pile by the windowsill.

Georgia nodded and flashed her a quick smile. "Thanks," she said, straightening her shoulders, confidence once again emanating from her. "I should be good."

"I've got a couple more things to do out back," Mel said. "Just call me if you need me."

Mel left Georgia in the office, and when she turned back to look, Georgia already had her nose buried in a file folder. Until moments ago, the idea of Georgia needing anyone seemed laughable. But Mel saw in her eyes the same flicker of vulnerability she'd seen at the pub the night before. Maybe the confidence was all a show. Whatever it was, a wave of desire to take care of Georgia had all but knocked her over.

Those dangerous thoughts needed to be quelled. Mel would finish her work and get to her clinic.

She opened the door and stepped back into the cool air out behind the shelter, breathing in the scent of the nearby pine trees that might soon be razed for some ridiculous development, or whatever else the city would be doing with this land. She sighed. Between that and Georgia's presence, she wasn't thinking straight.

Some more time with the animals would do her good. It always did.

Chapter Six

File by file, Georgia was more and more sunk. It wasn't just the animals who came to the shelter looking hungry or injured or as though they'd never felt a single moment of love in their lives, it was the stories that accompanied them: a fire that devastated a family's home, forcing them to give up their pet gecko while they lived in a motel; the bunnies found in a box outside the police station; the sheep and goat removed from a hobby farm after they were found with untreated ticks that had left them almost blind.

After an hour of reading and organizing, Georgia walked around the shelter, taking in the warm comfort of the environment, the clean surfaces, full food and water bowls, well-tended plants and natural light. Regardless of the circumstances that had brought them, the animals were safe and well taken care of here. She shuddered to think of the ones who weren't lucky enough to be brought in.

Many of them would be adopted, she knew, from the discharged files. But how did the system work? And what would happen to the rest of the animals who were still there once the shelter closed down?

She peered out the back window to see if Mel was still working out back, but she was nowhere to be seen. Looking out the front, she noticed Mel's truck was gone, and she was alone.

She checked her watch. She'd been there longer than necessary anyway, and Hayley would be by Nina's in an hour to take photos for the listing.

A coffee in town, then she'd head home.

The whir of the espresso machine and a waft of fresh-baked buttery scones greeted Georgia as she stepped into Rise and Grind. The interior was well designed and homey, with lattice woodworking on the wall, a high ceiling and a number of hanging plants. She thought about the coffee shop she frequented near her home on her way to work: all sleek lines and neon, a space that could double as an Apple store or the lobby of a modern hotel.

"You're back!" said the perky barista who had served Georgia the large dark roast she'd picked up on her way to the shelter that morning.

"One's not enough for today," Georgia said. "I'll

take a cappuccino this time." She peered at the selection of pastries behind glass. This couldn't become a habit. But just today. "And a slice of lemon cake."

The barista winked and slid the cake into a brown paper sleeve. "My favorite."

Georgia looked at her name tag. "Anna. Do you know Seamus O'Brien?"

"Seamus? Of course. I was wondering where he'd been. He always comes here at lunch for a peppermint tea, but we haven't seen him for a few days."

"He hurt his back, so he's been at home," Georgia said. "Do you know where he lives? I'd like to send him something. Something tells me he's not one for flowers, but maybe a box of your pastries would cheer him up."

"Of course. I don't know his address, but my dad is in his bridge group. I'll have him drop them off."

"Great," Georgia said.

"How do you know Seamus?" Anna asked.

"I'm volunteering at the shelter."

Anna sighed. "Ugh. I can't believe they're talking about shutting it down."

"Seriously," Georgia said. "I can't believe it either. It's a really special place."

"That's where Sam and I got Bingo," Anna said, pointing to a picture of a black cat behind the espresso machine. "I don't know what I'd do without him."

"Cute," Georgia said. She picked up her wallet. "Put a box of peppermint tea in there too, will you?"

she asked, then paid the bill. Poor Seamus. Not only was he laid up on his back, but he was about to lose his life's work. Talk about when it rains it pours.

She knew how that felt.

Back at Nina's, Georgia put away the dishes she'd set on the rack earlier to dry, straightened the tea towel, fluffed some pillows and got everything ready for Hayley's arrival.

Her phone dinged and she picked it up to find an email invitation for a video call with Mario and the other two execs, later that day, at 7 p.m.—4 p.m. LA time.

Suddenly, her mind was spinning. She had just a few hours to get prepared to convince her bosses that she was mentally and emotionally fit to return to Herstein PR, undo the damage she'd done and get back to the business of building her career.

She took a deep breath and gazed out at the stillness of the lake and the gentle ripple of wind sweeping across the water, trying to envision herself back in the boardroom, shoulders back, chin up, adrenaline rushing as she powered through an important deal. Negotiating with a celebrity tattle blog to keep an athlete's bathroom vaping pics under wraps. Smoothing over a suspected past affair between two TV co-stars by manipulating the timeline of their tryst. Going head-to-head with a journalist insinuating that a tech CEO was involved in a cryptocurrency Ponzi scheme.

In the months leading up to the video, Georgia had become more and more emboldened. She recalled one evening after work, having drinks at the Soho House West Hollywood and gazing out at the bright lights of the city below, daring the universe to send her a problem she couldn't solve.

How foolish she'd been.

And standing here, in a small cottage in Sunset County, she couldn't seem to summon that same winning mentality. Was there a chance she wouldn't have it for the meeting? The thought of facing a screen of serious, scrutinizing faces would have lit a fire under her in other circumstances. Now, with her chest tight and something catching in her throat, she felt like she would be fighting to breathe, never mind fighting for her job.

Her reverie was interrupted by a knock on the door. Hayley and the photographer came in and started to set up to do their thing. "I'll get out of your way," said Georgia, pulling on her jacket. A walk in the woods would do her good. After the walk, she'd call Paulina. Have a few laughs. Loosen up for the video meeting.

When she exited the cottage, the sun was hidden behind the clouds, and it felt cooler than it had earlier that morning at the shelter.

She picked up her pace to a brisk walk, trying to

get her heart rate up and warm up a bit. After several minutes, she recognized the cluster of birch trees that signaled she was close to Mel's place again.

When she'd found Mel in the back of the shelter that morning, Georgia wished she hadn't made such a loud entrance. She would have liked to have spent a moment or two watching Mel with the animals, seeing her in her element and exuding the nurture and care she had for the animals in her charge.

The breeze picked up, and a gentle mist started to fall. Georgia pulled her hood on, cursing herself for not bringing an umbrella. It wasn't an accessory she was used to thinking about at home.

As though the thought of Mel had conjured her out of thin air, Georgia looked up to see Mel walking toward her, on the other side of the road, Franny bounding ahead. She had changed out of her work clothes and had on a pair of dark jeans and a navy blue windbreaker. She also had an umbrella.

Georgia gave Mel a quick wave as they approached each other. Did Mel think Georgia was stalking her? And had she subconsciously gone this way on purpose, for the chance of this very meeting?

"I made it through all the files," Georgia said, as soon as Mel was within earshot. "You'll have to come up with another special task for me tomorrow."

"That was quick," Mel said. "Alright. I'll figure something out." The drizzle started to turn to light rain. "You're not dressed for the weather."

"I'm fine," Georgia said, wondering if her mascara had started to run down her face. "My real estate agent is at Nina's place with a photographer. So I'm just out for a few minutes to give them some room to do their thing."

Mel looked at her watch. "I don't have to be back at the office for another hour or so. If you don't want to go back to your place, you're welcome to come sit at mine for a few minutes. Get out of the rain. I don't have coffee, though."

Georgia considered. Go into Mel's house? Of course, she was dying to see it. And spend some time with Mel in a non-work setting. But what about the promise she'd made to herself that getting any closer to Mel Carter was a very bad idea? A distraction from the upcoming meeting that could help get her career back on track.

Then again, she was about to get soaked to the bone.

"Sure," Georgia said. "That's nice of you."

Mel motioned the way just as the sky opened up and it started to pour. They picked up their speed from a brisk walk to a quick jog, Franny leading the way.

When they reached Mel's front door, she held it open for Georgia, welcoming her into a clean, modern front foyer that wouldn't have been totally out of place in LA, save for the picture windows and skylights that looked out at the tall sycamores and black walnut trees instead of bougainvillea and jacarandas. Mel unleashed Franny, who bounded down the hallway, returning moments later with a rope toy, which she dropped at Georgia's feet.

"Look at that, she knows you're an animal expert," Mel said. Georgia tossed the toy down the hallway, gleaming hardwood floors with a woven runner leading to what looked like a bright kitchen. The house was as beautiful inside as it was outside. Being in Mel's house suddenly awoke some unexpected nerves, and she waited for Mel to give some indication of what to do next.

Mel looked down at herself, then at Georgia, and they both started laughing. "You're completely soaked," she said. "Let me get you a blanket. Or a change of clothes or something."

"It's not too bad," Georgia said, wiggling out of her jacket. She passed it to Mel, who put it on a hanger in the closet. "My sweater's dry underneath. And I can deal with some wet socks."

"Hold on a sec, I'll be right back," Mel said, disappearing down the hall.

Georgia stood alone in the foyer for a moment, taking in the space. The sparse decor, the clean lines and muted colors—the interior of her home was just as unknowable as Mel herself.

Mel appeared a moment later holding a gray fleece blanket. Georgia reached out to accept it, but Mel was already unfolding it and wrapping it around her shoulders.

"Thank you," Georgia said, grateful for the warmth.

Mel was so close that Georgia could pick up on a faint smell of her soap or something—what was it? Jasmine? Georgia shivered, slowly warming up but unable to control the jolting charge of having Mel tending to her.

"Come on in," Mel said. "I'll make you some tea."

Georgia followed her down the hallway to the kitchen, another clean, modern space, with gleaming marble countertops, a wide island surrounded by stools and a Miele range. Georgia took a seat at the island and watched as Mel turned on the kettle. "Chamomile tea okay?" she asked. "Sorry, no caffeine in it."

"Sure," Georgia said. "Speaking of caffeine, I was at the coffee shop today. The woman there told me that everyone in town was upset about the shelter getting shut down. Couldn't people pull together to save it?"

She could only see Mel's profile as she poked around in a cupboard, but it was enough to see her expression darken. Georgia had hit a nerve.

Mel pulled the tea canister out of the cupboard, then two mugs. She handled the items in her kitchen the same way as she did her tools at the shelter. Carefully, methodically. What would it feel like to be handled by Mel? The thought of Mel touching her, purposefully, intently, sent a shiver of pleasure through her. She tightened the blanket around her shoulders.

"Yeah," Mel said, "we'll see. It would take more

than a few community donations. And it could be good timing, at the end of the day. Seamus is getting old."

"But what about the animals? Where will they go?"

"We'll do our best to place them or see if another shelter in a nearby town has any room."

"And if not?" Georgia said.

Mel looked at her but didn't say anything, which told her everything she needed to know.

"Sorry. I don't mean to pry," Georgia said. Some guest she was, dripping all over the hardwood in the entranceway then dampening the mood by bringing up something that of course would be upsetting for Mel. Time to change the subject. "So how long have you lived here?" she asked, looking around the kitchen. "It's a stunning home."

"Two and a half years," Mel said. "And thanks. We like it here."

We? Did she have a girlfriend? Wife?

"Me and Franny," Mel said, a slight grin on her face. Of course.

"Have you always lived in town? Or do you mean you moved here three years ago?"

"Twenty questions, eh?" Mel said, pouring the kettle. She had pulled up the sleeves on her sweater to reveal her toned forearms.

"Sorry. It's what I do. I get to know people really well for a living."

"Marketing, was it?" Mel said. She passed Georgia her tea.

"PR. Mostly crisis management. So, if I take on a client I need to know them inside and out. Especially when they've done something wrong."

Mel perched on a stool on the other side of the island. She took her tea bag out of her mug and placed it in a saucer, then took a sip. "Well. You can question all you want. But I think you'll find I'm pretty straight and narrow."

Was Mel telling the truth? Or was this guard she had up there to hide something unscrupulous about her past? "Everyone has a skeleton or two, don't they?" Georgia said, observing her closely.

"Guess it depends on what you consider to be in the category of 'wrong.'"

Aha. People who had secrets always lived with a gray-area definition of what was bad behavior. "With my clients?" Georgia said. "Well, wrong can take many forms. Twitter tirades. Drug busts. Paying off SAT tutors to get their kids into Ivy League schools. 'Accidental' wardrobe malfunctions. Infidelity seems to top the list, though." She noticed Mel bristled at her last words. Had Mel cheated on someone? For some reason, it seemed unlikely. There was something principled about her that Georgia was latching on to.

"So, what, you like spending your time helping people cover up the stupid things they do?" Mel asked. Franny sauntered into the kitchen and put her head in Mel's lap, looking up at her with big puppy dog eyes, like she could stare at Mel all day. Georgia could relate.

"Everyone makes mistakes," Georgia continued. "But for people in the public eye, one mistake can cost an entire career. And the punishment doesn't always fit the deed."

"Huh," Mel said. She scratched Franny behind the ears, and the dog closed her eyes with pure joy. "So mistakes don't deserve to be punished?"

"I take it you don't agree?" Georgia said. She suddenly felt on the hot seat, and that even though they were speaking in generalities, whatever Mel was about to say was somehow directed at her.

"I just think there are too many people in the world who do bad things, knowing full well that what they're doing is wrong. And they're happy to get away with it, without any moral quandary."

Georgia took a sip of her tea, her cheeks burning. She cared a lot what Mel thought of her. Too much. "You may be right. But at the end of the day, it pays the bills."

"Well, that's important," Mel said. "But does it make you happy?"

There were many feelings Georgia associated with her job. Power. Accomplishment. Respect (usually). Being envied. Assurance that she could do hard things. And be damn good at them. But happiness? Did anyone really think that a job was supposed to make you *happy*? A job was supposed to be the thing that got you to a place where you could eventually do all the things in your personal life that made you happy.

"You still there?" Mel asked, and Georgia looked up from her tea.

She gave Mel a quick smile. "Happy? Of course. Well, until recently."

"How did you get into the PR field?"

"I've always been fascinated by people in the public eye. The larger-than-life personalities, the big, bold ideas. The money. When I was at Northwestern, I got a job in catering in the university president's office. That's where they entertained government figures, visiting professors and celebrities getting honorary degrees."

She remembered how every Sunday she would pore over the guest lists for the week ahead and spend hours studying the backgrounds of the visiting dignitaries, the research they were involved in or the companies they helmed, so that if there was even one moment of casual interaction, she'd have something smart to say. Between that and her own studies in languages and art history, she soon became a favorite, and it wasn't long before she'd been recommended by a visiting Silicon Valley executive to his PR team. She'd made a name for herself quickly, eventually attracting the attention of Mario Kimpton.

Mel sipped her tea from a bright yellow mug with a Cornell logo on it.

"Cornell grad?" Georgia said.

"Conference attendee. And don't change the subject. We were talking about your job. And why it only made you happy until recently."

"I didn't realize I was coming here for a therapy session," Georgia said.

Mel raised an eyebrow. "We don't have to talk about your job. But usually people don't share things like that unless it's a path they're willing to go down."

Georgia shifted in her seat. Mel had been hot and cold since the day she first met her. But now, sitting in the quiet of her kitchen while she gazed at Georgia intently, it was clear that Mel wasn't trying to make Georgia feel bad. She was listening to her in a way that told her she actually cared about what Georgia was saying, which was a tad unnerving, but at the same time, felt really good. "Okay. Well. Basically, I've been a walking stress bomb since the moment I started working at my company, and then my aunt Nina died, and then I lost my mind on a reporter on a red carpet because he was being a totally sexist idiot and I flung a tennis star's drink at him but he ducked and it hit Aurelia Martin. You've heard of her, right?"

Mel blinked, and Georgia burst out laughing at her stunned appearance.

"Wait, you're joking, right? I have a huge crush on her. She's one of the only celebrities I know."

"Not joking. There's video evidence all over the internet. That's what your hockey team had all seen."

Georgia paused, enjoying the look on Mel's face as she seemed to grapple with whether or not Georgia was pulling her leg.

"Okay," she said. "Well, that was a lot."

"A whole lot. A lot enough to get my bosses to force me to take a leave, and for Aurelia to threaten to press charges." There. She'd said it. She waited for Mel to scoff and point out the irony in the situation.

Instead, Mel's expression softened. "And you're dealing with that while you're also settling your aunt's affairs."

"Yup," Georgia said, raising her mug. "When it rains, it pours!"

Mel chuckled, and they both looked out the window to see that the sun was starting to poke back through the clouds.

"I've got a meeting later today with my bosses. Hopefully it's good news. So, now that you know all the skeletons in my closet," Georgia said, taking the last sip of her tea. "Surely you have something for me?"

"Sorry," Mel said. "Aside from a few high school hijinks that ended up with after-school detention, and two or three unpaid parking tickets..."

"Well, now that seems unfair. Now I'm the resident delinquent of the Sunset County animal shelter."

"I'll get you a badge," Mel said. She looked at her watch. "Do you want me to drive you back to your place? I've got an appointment I need to get back to the clinic for."

Suddenly Georgia felt foolish for sharing so much with Mel. Was she trying to get her out of there? "No, no, I'm good. Hayley should be finishing up soon, so I'll walk back."

Mel collected Georgia's mug and put it in the sink, then walked her to the entranceway, Franny trailing behind. "Here, take this," she said, passing her the umbrella.

"It's not raining anymore," Georgia said, passing it back. But she'd noted the sweet gesture.

"You never know when you'll run into trouble. You can bring it back to the shelter tomorrow."

Who was this new Mel? Georgia accepted the umbrella. "Okay. Thanks."

"And listen. What you said." Mel paused, and crossed her arms, leaning up against the wall. "I wouldn't consider that 'wrong.' You had an emotional response during a really hard time in your life. Maybe cut yourself a bit of slack."

Mel's words melted all over her like a soothing balm. "I appreciate that. It might be a little easier to do without a million people commenting on what a loose cannon I am."

"People can say all kinds of things hiding behind their computers. They don't count."

"They count when your job is hanging in the balance," Georgia said, but knowing it was of little consequence to Mel seemed like the only thing that really mattered in that moment. "But thanks."

"And hey. If your bosses need a reference, tell them to give me a call."

Georgia grinned. "I'll keep that in mind. Sometimes it feels like I'm working with a bunch of animals, with the clients I have. No offense, of course," she said to Franny, bending over to scratch behind her ears. She stood for a moment before reaching for the door handle. What she really wanted was to be wrapped up in a giant hug from Mel. She hadn't felt this understood, this cared for, in who knew how long. But even though Mel had started to open up, there was still some kind of weird barrier between them, and Georgia had no idea if a hug would be reciprocated.

Instead, she smiled and waved as she let herself out through the door, then headed back toward the road to Nina's, sensing Mel's eyes on her as she left.

Georgia arrived back at the cottage just as Hayley and the photographer were getting in their cars. "Hey," Hayley called as Georgia turned onto the driveway. "I was getting worried about you. That was some rain."

"Yeah, luckily I ran into Mel. We ducked into her place for tea."

"Oh," Hayley said, raising an eyebrow. "How lucky. Mel's not exactly known for rolling out the welcome mat."

"It was no big deal. We were right by her place, and I think she was just being neighborly."

Hayley smiled a knowing smile. "Chivalrous," she said. "I'm sure she loves having you at the shelter. You're just her type. Someone who might break her single streak. Many have tried."

"And? What's the story there?" Georgia tried once again to appear nonchalant. Could Hayley just give her something already?

"She's always been a bit of a closed book," Hayley said, a funny look on her face. She cleared her throat. Damn it. Georgia could tell that was all she'd be getting.

"Well, I'd love to go out again sometime," Georgia said. Maybe a couple more drinks would get Hayley talking.

"I'm sure we'll be celebrating your sale soon. Check out these shots that Jeremy just took. Of course, he'll do some editing and touch-ups, but take a look at a few of the raw files."

Hayley passed Georgia her iPad, and she scrolled through some of the images for the listing. She had to admit, it did look like a cozy and idyllic home for someone wanting to live in the peace of nature. A pang of sadness hit her at the idea of someone else living in Nina's home, the place where she'd passed the last days of her quiet, humble life.

"These are great," she said, passing the iPad back

to Hayley. "Thanks for all your work. I wouldn't have known where to start."

"My pleasure. So. The listing should be ready to go up on Monday. How does that work for you? Viewings through the week, and hopefully offers early the next. I've heard from some colleagues that there have been a ton of hopeful cottage-owners coming through recently. I think the opening of the Briarwood Inn over on Shaughnessy Lake last year and all the profiles of the up-and-coming food and craft beer scene have made this spot really exciting for families and investors. I wouldn't be surprised if we get multiple offers. Maybe even a bidding war."

"We like bidding wars," Georgia said, trying to feign enthusiasm. Obviously, she had to sell Nina's cottage. But something about the space over the last week, the way it felt so comfortable and safe as a place to lick her wounds and heal, well, Georgia was starting to understand what the word "home" really meant. How weird was that, that a place she'd never been, so far away from her own life, felt so much like home?

It's Nina, she reminded herself.

She bid farewell to Hayley, and after kicking off her shoes and changing out of her damp clothes, she flopped on her favorite spot on the green corduroy couch, grateful to have won the staging battle with Hayley. She gazed out the window to the lake, mind flitting between Nina, her job and what Hayley had said (and not said) about Mel. She checked her watch. One more hour until the phone call.

She willed her mind to quiet, lulled into a peaceful state gazing at the ripples on the water, ablaze with the orangey hue of the setting sun.

Sunset County. It was living up to its name.

Georgia stared out the window, rehearsing what she would say to Mario, Liz and Viola, who she knew would be skeptical about welcoming her back into the fold. Mario was likely on her side. But the other two? Even before everything that had unfolded, she sensed she still hadn't quite proven herself to Mario's partners.

After carefully styling her hair in loose waves and applying a healthy dose of under-eye concealer, she buttoned up a crisp white dress shirt and looked at herself in the mirror. Something was missing.

In the dining area, she dug through the box of Nina's things that she planned to take home until she found the small jewelry case. Nina wasn't much of a jewelry wearer, but in a small velvet pouch Georgia found a gold sand dollar pendant on a delicate chain that Georgia remembered on Nina. When she fastened it around her neck, her confidence ticked up ever so slightly.

"Here goes nothing," she whispered as she flipped open her laptop, adjusting the screen to capture her at her best angle.

She took a deep breath, then clicked on the video

meeting link from Mario's assistant. A message popped up on the screen that she was being held in a waiting room. She sat imagining the pre-meeting conversation that was going on at the moment. Deep breaths.

Suddenly, she saw her own face on the screen, and then she was joined by Mario, Liz and Viola, all with poker faces, hard to read even with the high resolution of her computer screen.

"Hi, everyone!" she said. *Ugh, too perky. Take it down a notch.*

"Georgia," Mario said. "Nice to see you. How are things in…where is it you're staying again?" He was leaning back in his Herman Miller office chair, facing what Georgia knew was a sweeping view of the LA city skyline, high enough to see all the way down to the Santa Monica Pier.

An office like the one she dreamed of occupying one day.

"Sunset County," Georgia said, angling her computer slightly so that the lake outside would be in the background. "I'm staying at my aunt's place. In Canada."

"We heard," Viola said. "Sorry for your loss."

"Thank you," Georgia said. "It's been a good trip so far. I'm feeling a lot better. And definitely recharged and ready to come back." *Don't go overboard.* "I've been volunteering."

A thick pause filled the air.

"We understand that you've been going through a

lot," said Liz, as though she was carefully choosing her words. "But you should know that more than a few of our clients have called with concerns."

Georgia felt her pulse quicken. She had to get control of the situation. "Of course. I—"

"And I speak for the three of us when I say that I share their concerns. Our job is not to be public facing. We're invisible. Behind the scenes. We're the people who make our clients shine. And what happened…well, that was pretty much the opposite of invisible."

"I understand. And it will never happen again. It was just—"

"We've redistributed your client list for the time being," Mario said. She suddenly felt nauseated as he listed off her roster and the other agents who were taking on her work. Any semblance of control over the situation was falling through her fingertips. She was going to be fired. She knew it.

"Does this mean… Am I losing my job?"

Another pause. "You're not losing your job, Georgia." She searched Mario's expression. Was he being genuine? Liz and Viola were still stone-faced. "We think your focus now should be on getting better. Take some more time. Focus on you. And we'll reconnect next week."

She didn't want to wait until next week. She wanted assurance *now*. The sting of tears threatened to spill. But they wouldn't see her crack. "Got it," she said, trying to sound chipper. She forced a smile. "I can't wait to be back."

Mario, Liz and Viola signed off, and Georgia sat in her chair, staring straight ahead at her laptop screen.

Well, she wasn't toast. But it sure wasn't the home run she was looking for.

Chapter Seven

"I'm sorry, did I just hear you say the word *gala*?" Georgia said, and Mel immediately regretted saying anything. "I *gala* like no one you've ever met. I wrote the book on gala. Okay, me and Truman Capote. Tell me you've at *least* heard of the Black and White Ball. The most legendary party of all time. You're saying there's a *gala* here? How am I only finding out about this now?" Her eyes were bright as she leaped up from the ground, where she'd been playing with and training the bunnies again, something that seemed to have become her go-to despite the other tasks Mel had on her list.

"It's, uh, a yearly thing. Sort of a fundraiser for the shelter. It's painful. But we get most of our donations that night, so..."

"So what you're saying is that it's Sunset County's don't-miss event of the year?"

"Okay, okay, laugh it up," Mel said. "I know it's not one of those fancy parties you go to in LA, but people around here kinda like it. At least this year it'll pay to get some of the animals relocated."

Georgia's expression softened. "Well, I think we've found the perfect job for me. I'd love to help organize it!"

"You'll have to pry that job from my aunt Connie's cold dead hands," Mel said. "But, uh, you should come. If you're still in town. It's next weekend."

She watched as Georgia processed the information, and while the shelter fundraiser was Mel's least favorite event of the year, maybe even less so than pub night at The Hidden Oar with her hockey team, she was suddenly desperate for Georgia to agree to come. The event started to hold some appeal with the idea of her there, in a dress, lighting up the room in the way she was so incredibly good at doing.

"I'll be around next weekend. It might double as my going-away party. My aunt's place should have sold by then."

Mel swallowed hard, reconciling with the notion that Georgia was only a temporary presence in her life. How was it that this amazing woman had swept into her life so quickly, and was already on her way out?

And now Mel was sitting on the edge of her seat, waiting to hear if Georgia would be in attendance at a night of cheesy table centerpieces and silent raffles for prizes no one really needed or wanted. Not to mention at least three or four Sunset County residents taking full advantage of the open bar to the point that they had more than a few regrets the next morning.

"So why don't I get in touch with Connie?" Georgia said, sitting back down and scooping up Mr. Dimiglio, cradling him against her chest. "These types of events always require another set of hands."

"If you do, don't say I didn't warn you," Mel said. "The woman likes things her own way."

"I'm used to dealing with difficult personalities, remember?" Georgia said. "It's my specialty."

Mel turned to the sink, pretending to rearrange some bottles of feed and trying to hide the smile on her face. The idea of Georgia going head-to-head with her aunt Connie was amusing. Mel might even pay to watch. She grabbed her phone, and shared Connie's contact to Georgia's number. "Alright. Feel free to get in touch. You'll be surprised that she's married to Seamus."

"Well, I can't wait to meet her," Georgia said. "I'll call her as soon as I'm finished here with my babies."

Mel watched from the doorway for a moment as once again, Georgia wrapped her right around her little finger, the way she gently played with the animals, murmuring to them softly and praising them as they performed the tricks she was training them to do. "Everything going okay with getting your aunt's cottage on the market?" Mel asked. She needed to leave but once again was unable to tear herself away from Georgia's presence.

"I think so. Hayley is an amazing agent." She looked up, and it seemed to Mel that she was trying to gauge her reaction to hearing Lauren's sister's name. Had Hayley told Georgia what happened?

She kept a steady, neutral expression. "Yeah, she's great."

Georgia paused, but Mel wasn't giving her anything. "You were friends with her sister, right?"

"Best friends."

"What happened?"

Mel scratched her neck. "Oh, you know. She moved a few towns over. We grew apart a bit." *And now she's dead to me.*

"Do you miss her?"

"Yeah, sure. We had a lot of history together, actually." *And not all the good kind.* Time to change the subject.

"Do you think you'll ever call her?"

Never. "Maybe. Would be nice to catch up." *Or horrible.* "Anyway, her sister seems like a really good agent." To be fair, Mel had always liked Lauren's kid sister, one of the few younger siblings of her friends who wasn't annoying and was sometimes even fun to be around. She'd follow them to the park and hit fly balls for them to catch, and although they tried to hide it, she was often the brave one when it came to catching and handling all manner of insects or frogs.

It seemed like Hayley was doing well for herself, and Mel wasn't surprised. Seeing her, though, and hearing about her in conversation still managed to bring back a rush of unpleasant feelings. Mel remembered seeing her at Breanne's funeral, seemingly put out that Mel wasn't speaking to Lauren or her family. Little did Hayley know it had taken everything inside of Mel to even show her face, and to this day she wasn't sure that it had been the right decision. The time had been marred with complicated, hazy choices, and all she could do was put one foot in front of the other and try to do the right thing.

Aside from Hayley's family and Seamus, whom Mel had confided in one night over a beer at the pub, no one knew about Breanne and Lauren's betrayal. People already felt sorry enough for Mel after Breanne died; there was no need to add their pity to the mix.

"I'm glad it's working out," Mel said. "It's a beautiful little place. One of the few remaining original structures in the area."

"Yeah. I didn't know how I'd like it there, since it's so quiet and secluded. Not really what I'm used to. But I can see the appeal for Nina." Georgia's bright light dimmed slightly.

"Are you looking forward to getting back to the

excitement of home?" Once again, the idea of Georgia leaving was anything but exciting to Mel. It was a punch in the gut.

"A little less now that I have a gala to look forward to!" she said. She grinned her thousand-watt grin, and all Mel could see was a picture in her mind of her picking Georgia up at Nina's, Georgia sliding into her car, then walking arm in arm together into the event.

Which she'd obviously never do. The thing with small towns was that the rumor mill worked at warp speed, maybe even faster than where Georgia came from, and the last thing Mel wanted was any of that type of attention. "Well, don't get your hopes up too high," she said, a refrain that had become her mantra over the last few years.

"High hopes? They get me out of bed every morning," Georgia said. "We can't all be cool and practical like you."

"Cool and practical, eh? Wait until you see me on the dance floor," Mel said, then exited to the sound of Georgia laughing.

"Dance floor?" Georgia called as Mel strode down the hall, unable to stop the wide smile that spread across her face. "I'll believe it when I see it!"

She was right. No way, no how, would she ever end up on the dance floor of the Sunset County Animal Shelter fundraiser. Or any dance floor for that matter. But the suggestion of it was enough to make

Georgia laugh, lighting up the halls of the shelter as Mel left for the second, and much less interesting, part of her day. And that felt pretty darn good.

Georgia thumbed through the files of two new residents of the shelter, a pair of miniature schnauzers dropped off that morning by the son of an elderly resident who had passed away a few days ago. Mel had stayed to do the intake, and after she left, Georgia spent a few minutes petting Salt and Pepper, who appeared to be healthy but completely starved for affection.

She read through their medical history and a few notes about their general demeanor, the food they were used to eating and the breeder they'd come from.

There was no doubt that these two dogs would make a beloved addition to the right family. As she looked at them, she thought about what she would look for in a pet. As adorable as they were, a dog would be out of the question. Not only would her work hours make walking a dog challenging, but the idea of that type of mess really didn't hold any appeal. And then there was the drooling.

"You're cute, but you're not for me," she whispered. "But I know you'll make someone else really happy. Now we just have to find you that someone else."

She picked up a notepad from the desk and jotted down a few phrases.

Double the love.

Nothing's complete without a dash of Salt and Pepper.

#WowzersSchnauzers

She smiled to herself at the idea of her being a PR agent to the adorable puppies, helping them put their best foot forward in order to find the right home. It was almost like helping her clients land on messaging for a challenging interview, or craft a public apology to post on social media, except these little cuties were made up of pure, fluffy innocence.

How could she get the message out about these two? Or any of the other animals that were in need of a home? The idea was even more urgent the more she thought about the shelter closing.

Georgia picked up her phone and searched the shelter's website. The page featured a basic setup, with contact information and some poorly shot photographs that made the animals look more like convicts than potential best friends or companions.

She sat back in her chair and pulled up her Instagram, to see if on the off chance, the shelter had a social media account. As she expected, it did not. Mel seemed proud of her social media aversion. Seamus certainly didn't seem like the type to be posting selfies and memes.

"You just need a spotlight," Georgia murmured to the schnauzers, bending down to pet them both behind the ears, their little stubby tails wagging in delight. She opened her camera app and snapped a few photos until she captured a perfect image of Salt nuzzling Pepper's neck. "Perfect," she whispered, another project blossoming in her mind.

After tidying up, gathering her things and then typing in the code on the digital lock pad, Georgia emerged into the sunny early afternoon, contemplating how to spend the rest of her day. There wasn't much more to do at Nina's aside from meeting with the lawyer to tie up some loose ends with her estate, but that meeting was set for Friday afternoon.

She could go·for a long hike. Or sink into the corduroy couch with a good book.

Instead, she ordered a latté at Rise and Grind and settled in at a table to make a phone call.

Her call was answered after one ring. "Connie here. Go."

Georgia stifled a laugh. She was used to this type of intensity in LA, where everyone seemed to think that their time was infinitely more valuable than whatever concern you were calling with. Then again, who was she to say that a small-town senior couldn't boast the same attitude? In fact, she already loved Connie.

"Connie? It's Georgia O'Neill calling. I've been helping out at the shelter recently, and I understand there's a big event happening next weekend that you might need a hand with?"

The line was silent. "You mean the shelter fundraiser?"

Georgia sensed she was about to be shown the door before she even made a case for her experience and party-planning expertise. "The very one. I'm—"

"Well, thank goodness for you. Melanie said you might be calling. We're days away and I'm spending half of my time acting as a nurse for Seamus. And do you know that I've been telling him all these years to join me at the rec center even once a week? How does anyone think they're going to do anything in their golden years without a bit of a time and energy investment in their body?"

Georgia wanted to hug her through the phone. "Well, Connie, that's a great question. It sounds like you've got a lot going on over there." She couldn't wait to tell Mel that she'd been 100 percent wrong about Georgia's idea to get in touch with her aunt.

"How are you at seating charts? I'll give you the rundown of who's who in this town. And I'll need a hand with the timing of events. Hors d'oeuvres, speakers, etc."

As Georgia listened to the laundry list of tasks that Connie needed help with, she suddenly wondered how she would fit everything in with the sale of Nina's place, getting back into the good graces of her bosses and the new publicity project she couldn't wait to get started on.

How was it that she was sent away for some R & R, and within days had managed to find herself with too much on her plate?

"I'm on it, Connie," Georgia said. "Why don't I swing by your place on Saturday and we can talk details? Just let me know your address."

It was her way. Georgia knew that she felt at her best when she was busy, and for the first time since she'd arrived in Sunset County, she realized she'd gone a whole several hours without thinking of what she'd done that had gotten her sent here. She might have even forgotten for a moment that she was miles and miles from home. The whole town of Sunset County was just as comfortable as Nina's couch, and she was relishing in the feeling of being wrapped in it like a big fuzzy blanket.

"Can you bring another box of those pastries while you're at it? Something to keep Seamus busy for at least a few minutes. He's driving me up the wall."

"You got it," Georgia said. Mel might have been wrong about Connie accepting her help, but she was right on the mark with the fact that based on the little that she knew about her, Connie and Seamus appeared to be a very unlikely couple.

She hung up her phone and spent a few minutes enjoying her latté, watching the steady stream of customers coming in and out, each known by name by the barista, Sam, who she now knew was also the owner, and husband of Anna.

The community board beside the coffee counter caught her eye, with advertisements for painting and tutoring services, the local library's creative writing contest, and a flyer with tear-off phone number tabs. She stood up to move closer.

Adopt a Kitten, the flyer read, with some contact information, a photograph and a brief blurb about the very same six adorably fluffy kittens Georgia had found under Nina's porch just over a week ago. Apparently the Harris family had decided that seven cats under one roof was indeed too many, and that they should see if any locals were interested in bringing home one of the litter. The sign must have been posted that day, as the kittens had already grown a bit. Right away, she picked out the little orange-and-white one who'd gotten stuck in her sweater, the feisty little kitten who seemed to march to the beat of his own drum.

Her heart swelled as she thought about the little kitten heading to a new home, separated from his brothers and sisters and mother, starting over anew in an unfamiliar place. She instinctively went to rip one of the phone number tabs from the bottom of the page, and then pulled back her hand.

She laughed to herself. A pet? Her?

Maybe there was something in the coffee in Sunset County.

Chapter Eight

Georgia was deep in a late-afternoon nap when a knock at the door startled her awake. She slid off the couch, quickly checked her appearance in the mirror and opened the front door to find Mel, who was wearing a black bomber and a pair of aviators. *Hello, doctor*, Georgia thought as she took in the knockout of a woman in front of her, suddenly self-conscious of her own disheveled appearance. Was she dreaming?

She thought of the trouble she'd been going to before her shifts at the shelter, a casual, effortless look that definitely took more time behind-the-scenes than it might have appeared.

"Mel," Georgia said, emerging from the fog of her nap. "Everything okay?" Had she left the door to the shelter unlocked? Or was Mel coming to admit she was wrong about Connie?

"I was just driving by on my way home from the clinic and thought you might have some insight into why we've received six calls in the past two hours about adopting Salt and Pepper. And as a duo, specifically."

Georgia gasped. "It worked!" It took everything in her not to hug Mel. The idea of it, of being pressed up against her firm, athletic body, was even more exciting than the news Mel had come to deliver.

"What worked? What did you do?"

"Why don't you come in?" Georgia asked, racking her brain and trying to remember if she had something in the fridge to offer. Would it have killed Mel to give her some advance notice?

Mel stepped into the front entranceway, surveying the inside of the cottage. "Great place," she said. "Hope the new owners don't do too much remodeling. I've always loved the original detail in these cottages."

"Well, if they're willing to pay the right price, I don't have too much input into what they do with it after that. But yeah, it's nice." She looked around, seeing Nina's cottage through new eyes. When she'd arrived in Sunset County, she'd found the place quaint and maybe a bit charming, but not something she would have chosen for herself. Now, after a few weeks being at the cottage, and observing as Mel took in the original details and craftsmanship, she knew that that Nina's place was a truly special one. "Can I get you anything? A glass of wine? A beer? You're off the clock, right? Or do you not drink?"

Mel turned to look at her, amusement all over her face. "You clearly think I'm a total wet blanket."

"Nope. You've promised to own the dance floor next weekend, remember?"

Mel laughed, her brown eyes locked on to Georgia's in a way that made her heart skip a beat. "You know it. Yeah, sure, I'll have a beer."

"Why don't you grab a seat in the living room? I'll be right there."

In the kitchen, Georgia took a moment to finger comb her hair and apply a light coat of lip gloss. She poured some cashews in a small bowl and then grabbed two beers from the fridge.

"So," Mel said, accepting the beer and clinking it against Georgia's. "Explain to me how you had a hand in what might be the fastest adoption we've ever done."

"Well, I noticed this morning that the shelter doesn't have an Instagram account."

"Why would we need an Instagram account? We're an animal shelter, not a fifteen-year-old girl."

Georgia grinned. She couldn't imagine existing in a world so cut off from the realm of social media, but it was kind of cute that Mel did. Not only that, but she also liked what it said about her values. "Well, listen. Social media just provided you with six potential families for Salt and Pepper. So I guess it's not all that frivolous."

"Alright, show me what you put on there."

Georgia tapped her passcode on her phone, then pulled up the @SunsetCountyAnimalShelter account she'd created that afternoon. The only entry was the adorable photo of Salt and Pepper nuzzling each other, accompanied by a tagline Georgia had written and some strategic hashtags that she knew would direct the message toward people who lived in Sunset County and the surrounding communities. She moved closer to Mel, close enough that they were touching. Mel didn't move away.

"This is really funny," Mel said, looking sideways at her, and Georgia noticed an adorable faint sprinkling of freckles across Mel's nose.

"So…why aren't you laughing?" Georgia said. She shifted slightly in her seat so that she was facing Mel. There was lots of room on the old corduroy couch, but Georgia was happy they weren't making use of it.

Mel was quiet for a moment, then she looked back at the photo and appeared to be rereading the caption. She looked back at Georgia, her face breaking into a wide smile. "What made you do this?"

She wasn't 100 percent sure, but she was pretty certain that Mel was okay with her going rogue, given the results. "I just stared deep into their little puppy eyes and got inspired," she said. Which was the truth. "Guess these little guys just needed some good PR."

Mel sat back in her seat, looking at Georgia quizzically. "And it seems like you gave it to them. Now we just need to figure out where they'll go. We've never been spoiled for choice like this."

Georgia took a swig of her drink, enjoying the same satisfaction she felt whenever she closed a big deal or smoothed over a challenging situation for a client. So what if she'd screwed up! She'd been hired at Herstein PR for a reason: she was damn good at her job. And she felt a rush of confidence in being able to showcase her talent to Mel.

The sudden spark made her bold. "Stay for dinner," Georgia said, more as a command than a question. One thing she knew about women like Mel was that although they might say they don't like being told what to do, secretly they responded well to a take-charge attitude.

Georgia gauged Mel's reaction to the invite, feeling some pins and needles in the seconds between when she made the request and the moment when Mel nodded her head, a funny expression on her face.

"Just don't tell me you're a vegan or something. I mean, if you are, we can order in. But I was planning on making carbonara, so…"

"Not a vegan. And as long as you'll let me help."

"You got it," Georgia said. Hours earlier she'd been in the grocery store deciding between the dinner she'd likely be having in LA—a simple boneless, skinless chicken breast and some steamed broccoli—and the more indulgent, infinitely more delicious pasta dish. Nina's voice had popped into her mind, and she'd thought *To hell with it.* Time to enjoy herself a bit. Now, with Mel as her surprise company for dinner, she was even more thrilled to have made that decision. She stood up and motioned to the kitchen. "Shall we?"

Half an hour later, wine had been poured, an old Al Green record was spinning on Nina's vinyl player, and Georgia and Mel were working side by side in Nina's kitchen, Georgia preparing the ingredients for a kale and Parmesan salad with lemon and garlic dressing, and Mel chopping a bunch of fresh parsley while thick pancetta simmered in water.

"You seem to know your way around the kitchen," Georgia said, eyeing how easily Mel handled the chef's knife.

"I worked as a line cook at a restaurant to help pay for my undergrad. The head chef ran a real tight ship. It was hard work, but I learned a lot." She swept the chopped parsley to the side of the cutting board with a flourish, then removed the pancetta from the stovetop and set about slicing it into uniform cubes. "Turns out I love to cook."

"Ugh. I wish I did," Georgia said, hoping Mel wouldn't judge her much less refined chopping skills as she sliced the kale into uneven ribbons. "Seriously. My Uber Eats bill tells quite the tale. It's that, or something bland that I can steam in like fifteen minutes."

"So what inspired tonight's dinner? Just waiting for a stranger to come off the street?"

"Just have a bit more time on my hands these days. So."

Mel put her knife down on the cutting board, then wiped her hands on the dish towel that Georgia passed her. She leaned against the counter, then plucked a cherry tomato from Georgia's cutting board and popped it in her mouth. "Wait. So, you're volunteering at the shelter. Somehow you've convinced Connie to let you help her with the fundraiser. You've taken on a new social media project, *and* you're settling your aunt's estate. Tell me how that equals time on your hands."

Georgia flashed her a quick smile. "You don't know what my schedule was like back in LA. To be honest this feels like a vacation in comparison. And I might just be a bit of a workaholic."

"Ah," said Mel. "Well, I can't say I'm shocked."

"What does that mean?"

Georgia looked up again from her cutting board to find Mel looking at her closely. "Nothing. It's not an insult. It's just that you're really efficient. And tuned in. It's impressive."

Georgia tried to suppress the wide grin that was threatening to blow her cover. What Mel had just said was exactly what she was dying to hear, and everything she'd worked so hard to project. Talk about being tuned in. And hearing it from Mel, someone who clearly wasn't quick to praise—well, that was just the icing on the cake.

"Relationship?" Mel asked.

"Not much of a relationship type." Georgia looked sideways at Mel to gauge her reaction. Did that slight, sexy upturn on one side of her mouth mean she was pleased?

"Too busy?" Mel said.

"Yup. Maybe in a few years, once I've got my dream job. Although that might mean just a whole other level of time commitment. Who knows." Mel's expression returned to neutral, but her gaze was fixed intently on Georgia as she sliced a baguette for the table.

A few more sips of wine, and Georgia could picture exactly what would happen next. She'd drop her knife on the cutting board. Then, she'd hook one finger in the belt loop of Mel's jeans and guide her against the counter. She'd slide a hand up her abdomen to her chest, where she'd pause for a moment, before trailing her fingers behind her neck, pulling Mel's face toward hers and melting into her delicious-looking lips.

Instead, Georgia shot Mel a quick smile, hoping she didn't notice the flush in her cheeks summoned by her quick daydream. *Was* it a daydream? Or was it more of a wish?

"I'm going to set the table," Georgia said. What was she thinking, entertaining the idea of Mel Carter? What, so she'd kiss her, and who knows what more, and then there would be an awkward week and a half left where she'd run into Mel at the shelter, where she was supposed to be a model volunteer, and then bid farewell to her and Sunset County? Or worse, it wouldn't be a one-off, and all of a sudden she'd be dealing with the type of distraction that would cause her to lose the razor edge she needed to nail her next meeting with her bosses.

Alone in the dining room, Georgia took a deep breath as she laid out the cutlery and cloth napkins from the buffet. She surveyed the table. They were definitely sitting too close. Close enough that their legs might brush under the table. And if their legs brushed, and there was contact, well, that was something Georgia couldn't really see herself not following up on. She picked up one table setting and moved it to the opposite side of the table. Best to play it safe.

"Should be ready," Mel's voice called from the kitchen. It was a strange feeling, cooking alongside someone, not sitting down to eat in front of the television. And she liked it. She really liked it, which was a problem.

Mel pulled the cast-iron pan off the element and glanced over her shoulder, waiting for Georgia to return to the kitchen. She thought about the strip loin sitting in her fridge that she'd been expecting to grill that evening. She'd seasoned it that morning, back when she still had her head on straight.

And now here she was, about to have dinner with Georgia, the two of them alone together, with a great bottle of wine, music and pasta. Like a date. How had she ended up basically on a date?

She'd be fooling herself if she said that she hadn't welcomed the excuse to drop by the cottage to see Georgia on her way home from the clinic. Of course, she was curious about how Georgia had managed to generate such quick interest in the schnauzers, but a phone call would have sufficed. The truth was, she needed to see her. And while she was driving home, the discipline and good sense on which she prided herself had disappeared in a cloud of smoke as she found herself turning in to the long lane that led to the cottage, and to the woman who was turning her into a version of herself she didn't know.

Polite conversation, help with dishes, then head home. And it was time to switch to water, not only because she had to drive back to her place. She needed to keep her wits about her in order to navigate the rest of the evening.

When Georgia reentered the kitchen, Mel kept an eye on her as she moved between the stove and the sink, swaying her hips as she hummed the song that was playing. Her top didn't quite reach the waistband of her jeans, giving Mel a glimpse of her slender waist, her soft skin begging to be touched—it would take everything in her to make it through the next hour. But she'd brought it upon herself.

"Smells great," Georgia said. "Thank goodness for you. I'd have made a mess of this dish. This is restaurant quality."

"Better try it first before you come to any conclusions," Mel said.

Georgia bit her lip. She was taunting Mel. She approached the stove, and peered at the contents of the cast-iron pan, then turned to look up at Mel with that delicious grin on her face. She leaned in a little further, and suddenly her body was pressed right up next to Mel's. As Mel grappled with what was happening, her mind racing faster than any capacity for physical reaction, she felt Georgia's body shift, then she stood back and held up the serving spoon that had been on the cutting board on the counter right behind Mel. "Well, let's eat," she said, eyes dancing with delight. She passed Mel the spoon.

Willing herself not to tremble, or worse, drop an entire spoonful on the floor, Mel served them each a portion of the pasta, then followed Georgia into the dining room, noting that she'd set their places at opposite sides of the table. Good.

"Bon appétit," Georgia said, raising her glass.

"Cheers," Mel said, still trying to maintain her composure. She had to act normal. "And thanks for dinner." Now it was really feeling like a date. Mel felt her skin temperature tick up ever higher, even though the fire in the living room had started to die out.

"It's nice to have some company."

The amber hue of the setting sun filled the dining room with a rich glow, and Mel took a moment to commit the scene to memory. How long had it been since she'd had dinner with a beautiful woman?

Memories from her relationship with Breanne flashed through her mind. The French bistro where they'd had their first date, and where they often went for birthdays and special occasions. The picnic they'd made while on vacation in Hawaii, which they'd waited until the end of a hike to unpack, sitting next to a waterfall. The steak house where they'd celebrated Breanne's thirtieth birthday with her family.

She winced at that memory, suddenly overcome by how foolish she'd been, in love with a woman who was unfaithful to her, ready to commit all of herself and her life to that farce.

She looked up from her plate, Georgia beaming at her from across the table, and all of a sudden she felt the weight of the decision to come here. She was falling for Georgia, there was no denying it. But it wasn't too late to turn back.

"I, uh, think I heard my phone. I'd better check it— emergency calls from the clinic are routed through." She excused herself and returned to the front entrance. She needed to make a quick escape. Every moment with Georgia O'Neill was a step in the wrong direction, a threat to undo her.

"Everything okay?" Georgia called from the dining room.

Mel grabbed her phone from her coat pocket. "I'm really sorry. Turns out I have to go," she said. She didn't like to lie, as a rule, but she didn't know any other way out. What was she supposed to do, go back in there and tell Georgia that being around her was like kryptonite, that she was so unbelievably attracted to her that she didn't trust herself anymore?

Better to break yet another one of her rules.

Georgia appeared in the entrance, a look of concern in her eyes. Or was it suspicion?

"Sorry," Mel said, holding up her phone. "Sounds like one of my client's dogs swallowed a sock. Should be okay but we're going to check her out just to be sure."

"Poor thing," Georgia said, and Mel was certain she detected disappointment in her voice. Was Georgia actually upset that she was leaving? "Here, I'll pack you something to go." She started rummaging around in a box near the door. "I thought I threw some Tupperware in here somewhere."

"You don't need to go to the trouble," Mel said, feeling even more guilty now and already regretting her lie. Regretting stopping by even more.

"Here!" she said, pulling a container out. "Don't

be silly. You made this amazing dinner. You can heat it up when you get home."

Mel watched as Georgia filled up the container, her long, silky hair brushing her collarbone so perfectly. How could someone be so alluring, so magnetic? It suddenly seemed impossible to willingly leave her side.

Georgia passed Mel the Tupperware, her hand brushing against hers, the warm feeling of her soft skin sending Mel's senses into overdrive. "Well, that was fun while it lasted," Georgia said, smiling that bright smile that made Mel feel like she could melt into the floor.

Georgia walked Mel to the front door, and she was keenly aware that she was leaving her to eat on her own. What kind of a jerk was she?

As though she could read Mel's mind, Georgia said, "Good thing I'm used to eating on my own. Lorelai and Rory will keep me company."

Mel gave her a confused look. Was she supposed to know what that meant?

"Oh, come on, you totally live under a rock. You've never heard of *Gilmore Girls*?"

"Actually, I think my sister is into that show. Maybe you two should hang out. Anyway, thanks again for this," she said, raising the container. "Have a good rest of the night."

As Mel passed Georgia on the way out the door,

the air filled with her alluring floral scent, tipping Mel
even further into sensory overload.

It might have been an abrupt exit. And downright
deceptive. But as Mel walked out of the cottage, certain that one more minute there with Georgia would
have been downright dangerous, she was certain her
decision was a smart one.

Chapter Nine

Before leaving the cottage for her shift at the shelter on Thursday morning, Georgia's phone dinged with a text from Hayley, letting her know that the draft of the real estate listing was ready for approval. Georgia pulled up the website and scanned through the description of the cottage and its features, and swiped through the photos.

A wave of sorrow washed over her. Going through Nina's keepsakes had been challenging, but the listing had a sense of finality to it, really emphasizing that she was putting this space up for sale, this space that carried so much of her beloved aunt's spirit, where she'd lived and had her most private hopes and dreams. It felt like the last place in the world that carried Nina's essence, and now Georgia was tossing it out to the world with a dollar value attached.

Try as she might, she couldn't contain the sob that overtook her, and hot tears flowed as she thought about strong, courageous Nina, who lived her life with such conviction and strength of purpose, and was robbed of it before even reaching her senior years.

She allowed for a few minutes of sadness before pulling herself together. Had she properly grieved her aunt? Did she even know the first thing about how to do that?

Her parents certainly had never taught her how to process her emotions. It was all about forging ahead, hitting the next goalpost.

That mindset had gotten her to where she was, but was of no value in moments like these, when she had to make sense of complicated feelings.

Driving to the shelter, she took deep breaths, trying to quiet the emotions that were all too real, all too raw. All she needed was some work to distract her. Hopefully, Mel would be at her clinic that morning, and Georgia could take a few minutes to compose herself before seeing her again.

No such luck. Mel's silver truck was parked right out front. She checked out her eyes in the rearview mirror, wiping away a small smudge of mascara. *Come on, Georgia. It's just a little shack in the woods.* Not to mention the fact that the money from the sale would be going directly to Aurelia Martin's charity, which she could feel genuinely good about.

She strode toward the entrance of the shelter, straightening her shoulders and willing the lump in her throat to disappear.

Except the moment she walked through the shelter door to find Mel with a woman and two small kids who were fawning over Salt and Pepper, excitement in their eyes, the lump only grew.

"Hey," Mel said. She looked at the woman. "That's Georgia. She made the post on Instagram."

"I'm Devyn," the dark-haired woman said. "Ella and Max's babysitter showed them the photo of Salt and Pepper last night. They begged to come and see them on our way to school."

Georgia tried to force a smile. "Oh, wow. That's great," she heard herself say. Looking at the happy children and their mom, and seeing Mel with a satisfied expression on her exquisite face, was too much for her to bear.

"I'm going to throw my coat in the back," she lied. She tried to move to the back room without attracting too much attention. Luckily, the family was far too engrossed with the dogs, but Mel caught her eye, and her change in expression made it clear she could sense her distress.

Georgia quickly retreated to the washroom, locking the door behind her as the tears spilled again. Why was she so upset? She was taking care of business. Finishing what Nina had asked her to do, and clearing up her own mess too. For goodness' sake. She had to get it together.

A few deep breaths and a splash of water on her face, and Georgia was ready to start her shift. Hopefully, Mel would be tied up for a few more minutes with the family, and she could get started without having to worry about the additional challenge of whatever had been in the air the night before at dinner.

She quietly exited the bathroom to the sound of the shelter's door chiming.

"Georgia?" Mel's voice called. No such luck.

"Hey," she called back, pausing for a moment in the hall and hoping Mel would stay out front. "Just going to head out and do the feed and water outside."

Mel appeared in the hallway, and by the concern in her eyes, Georgia knew right away that her efforts to mask her emotional outburst were for naught. She placed the bucket she was holding on the floor. The soft, light blue knit sweater she was wearing not only showcased her broad shoulders perfectly, but made them look like exactly the place Georgia wanted to bury her face and have a good cry. "What happened?" Mel said. "Is everything okay?"

She could lie, but what was the point? "No, actually. I saw the listing for Nina's place this morning, and I'm feeling really sad about it. And I'm still waiting to hear back from my bosses, and I have no idea what's going on with my future. And I'm out of my favorite waterproof mascara so basically today is the worst." She did her best to smile and add some levity to the moment, but Mel didn't bite.

Mel approached her, eyebrows furrowed. Georgia willed her to come closer, to take her in her arms and whisper that everything was going to be okay. What was happening to her? What was happening to the Georgia O'Neill who didn't need things like a shoulder to cry on?

Her tears pooled in her eyes again, and Georgia squeezed them shut, fingers pressing on her eyelids as though she could somehow stem the flow from her tear ducts.

"Hey, hey, it's okay." She heard Mel's steady and reassuring voice right beside her, close enough that she could almost reach out and grab her words.

She opened her eyes slightly, and through the hazy mist of her tears found Mel right in front of her. Unable to find words of her own, she watched as Mel reached out, placing her fingers on Georgia's cheek, lifting her face ever so slightly so that she was looking directly into her deep brown eyes. Mel's eyes searched hers. "What can I do to help?" Her authoritative, husky voice made Georgia tremble, and the care she spoke with made Georgia instinctively place her hand over Mel's fingers, as if to hold her there like a compress.

It was the first time Mel had really touched her. And even though it was just her fingers on her cheek,

Mel's skin against hers fired up every minuscule nerve ending in her body, sending heat shooting from her chin right down her torso and stirring up a burning desire.

Georgia leaned in to the touch, turning her chin ever so slightly and guiding the tips of Mel's fingers to softly graze the side of her face, leaving a tickle of electricity on her skin.

"Talk to me," Mel said. Her lips were barely parted, and Georgia watched as her chest started to rise and fall a little more quickly.

In that moment, the only thing that made sense to Georgia in the world was not talking at all, but kissing the lips that uttered those words. She opened her mouth slightly, knowing from the concerned, yet ravenous expression in Mel's eyes that she was thinking the very same thing.

Magnetic heat hung in the air as Mel's fingers trailed down Georgia's chin to the nape of her neck, where she slipped her hand under the collar of Georgia's sweater and pulled her closer, eyes fiery with desire. Georgia took the invitation, her lips meeting Mel's, melting into a luscious, tender kiss. She drew a deep breath, the lump that had been in her throat quickly disappearing with her quiet groan. Mel's lips moved slowly at first, until the tenderness between them turned to hunger.

Mel tasted delicious, a combination of fruity lip balm and peppermint, and her soft mouth moved with the same steadiness and authority that she radiated, directing the pace and pressure of the kiss. Georgia submitted easily to Mel's lead, her arousal multiplying with every flicker of Mel's tongue.

She let out a quiet, involuntary sigh as Mel's fingers traced the skin on the back of her neck, then slowly down the back of her sweater, to her waist, where she pulled Georgia even closer, until any space between them disappeared.

When Mel sucked on Georgia's lip, and she fluttered her eyes open long enough to lock in Mel's gaze, Georgia grabbed hold of her arms, feeling the impressive strength of her triceps even through her white lab coat. She was at once floating and feeling steadier and safer than ever.

When Mel suddenly pulled away, taking a deep breath in, Georgia wondered for a moment if she'd done something wrong, if in a moment of passion she'd kissed Mel instead of the other way around. Until she took in the desperate need in Mel's eyes. It was a look that told her if they were anywhere else, she wouldn't—couldn't—have stopped at a kiss.

But then Mel took a step back, and Georgia immediately felt the gap between them, like a cold canyon. "I'm sorry. I shouldn't have done that," she said, her voice gravelly and deep, strengthening the depth of the body buzz that had taken over Georgia's senses.

"You don't need to—"

"Yes, I do," Mel said, and suddenly she was moving farther away, when all Georgia wanted was to be back in her arms.

Georgia reached out and gripped Mel's hand, moving to pull her back. Her lips tingled, the feeling of Mel's hand at the nape of her neck lingering, her phantom fingers still moving through her hair so gently, the heat from her skin still a thick current of energy in the air. She steeled herself.

"This isn't a good idea," Mel said quietly, allowing Georgia to grasp her hand but not moving any closer.

Georgia's mind raced as quickly as her pulse. She wanted more. But was Mel the only one thinking clearly? "Okay," she said, detangling her fingers from Mel's. She ran them through her hair.

"I'm going to head out," Mel said, her voice still hoarse. "I'll see you later."

She made a move toward the reception area, then turned back to face Georgia. "Are you going to be okay?"

Georgia had almost forgotten about why she'd retreated to the back in the first place. She nodded and bit her bottom lip, which was still tingling.

Mel gave her a quick smile, the smooth skin of her cheeks flushed. She waved, and without another word, she was gone.

Georgia took a deep breath and held on to the wall for support.

So Mel was concerned they were being unprofessional. Sure, maybe a line had been crossed. But it wasn't like Mel was really her boss or anything. And she'd be leaving in a little over a week. And who knew? Maybe a bit of a fling would be good for them both.

The trouble was, Mel was making her feel all kinds of things beyond the thrill of the kiss. Things that she knew she needed to stay away from, if she ever hoped to harness the focus she needed to get her life back on track.

Fun was one thing. What she was feeling? Definitely a whole other ball game.

It had been a while since she'd been kissed. But she'd never, ever been kissed quite like that.

"We are the best!" Andie sighed as she and Mel stood back to admire their handiwork. "The boys are going to be thrilled. They should be home any second."

Mel had been at her sister's for the past three hours, helping to install bunk beds for her eight-year-old twin nephews, who would be home from a Friday overnight at their dad's anytime now. She turned to Andie, taking in the worn-out expression on her face and the fine lines near her eyes that she couldn't remember seeing until just recently. "You getting enough sleep?" Mel asked.

"Ugh, why don't you just come out and say it? I look rough," Andie said, flopping back on the bean-bag in the twins' room. "It's my lot in life. I'm finally at a place where I'm feeling good, got my shit together and, dare I say it, ready to start dating again, and I seem to have aged ten years overnight."

"Well, starting your own business isn't exactly synonymous with R & R," Mel said. Andie was opening a children's play center on Main Street in a month's time, and she'd been working around the clock to get the store ready with a calendar full of birthday party bookings, all while managing the bounding-with-energy twins. "Why don't you have a hot shower before the boys get in? I'll clean up here."

"Honestly?" Andie said, her tired eyes lighting up. "You really are the best. Speaking of dating—"

"We're not speaking of dating," Mel said, rolling her eyes. Without fail, her sister managed to broach the topic any time they were alone together. Andie was the only person who could get away with poking into her private life. But it didn't mean she had to engage.

"You're four years older than me, you know," Andie said, leaning in the doorway. "I might look tired, but you're getting legitimately old."

"I'm pretty sure I don't even classify as middle-aged," Mel said. "And there's more to life than dating. You're reading too many of those stupid magazines."

"Whatever you say," Andie said. "I'll go shower. Are you sticking around to see the boys?"

"I'll be here," Mel said. Seeing her nephews and her sister was always a high point in her week. The boys were a handful but a ton of fun to play with, and

Mel liked being able to give her sister a break for a few minutes by taking them to the park to shoot hoops or helping them with their schoolwork. Andie was a great mom, but she sometimes managed to mask how challenging it was to do alone. The boys went to their dad's for a night or two every second weekend, but Andie's ex, Greg, had a new wife and a new baby, and Mel knew that although the divorce had been amicable and they loved being with their dad, her presence in the boys' lives was important to them too.

Andie disappeared into the bathroom, and Mel set about folding the IKEA boxes and organizing the tools in the tool kit.

After everything was put away, she went to the kitchen to get a drink. She opened a can of sparkling water and took a long gulp, then stood in front of the fridge, looking at the collection of photos, drawings and notes held up by magnets.

A picture from the twins' fourth birthday caught her eye. She plucked it from the fridge, examining it more closely. The boys sat at the table with matching cakes in front of them. Matthew, the wilder of the two, already had icing on his face and was sporting a huge grin. Mel chuckled, remembering how he'd taken a swipe with his finger at the icing when Andie placed the cake in front of him, with no regard for the customary song and candle extinguishing that his mom was hoping to get on video. Ryan, who was just as lively but much more of a rule follower, was waving at the camera, his chubby cheeks ready to blow out the candles.

Mel's chest tightened when she remembered who had taken the photo. Breanne had designated herself the official photographer of the birthday party. Mel remembered this because her favorite photo of them was a selfie Breanne had taken, right after she dabbed a glob of icing on Mel's nose and kissed her on the cheek while Mel smiled a goofy, lovestruck grin into the camera. The photo had captured how funny the moment was, how light life had felt at the time and how smitten she'd been with the woman who'd broken her heart into pieces.

Mel pictured the photo, tucked into a small box of things she'd kept from their relationship. There was a good chance she would never get over the anger and betrayal. But something inside her wouldn't allow her to completely destroy the last memories of them together. Maybe it was self-preservation. A tangible warning in the event she ever started to make the mistake of wading down that path again.

She affixed the photo back onto the fridge, pushed away the memory of Breanne kissing her on the cheek, then thought for the millionth time that day about another kiss. The ill-advised, totally unprofessional, completely unavoidable and utterly unforgettable kiss between her and Georgia, only two days earlier, but that somehow, whenever she thought about it, felt like it had happened only moments ago.

With crystal clear accuracy she could summon the exact feeling of Georgia's velvety lips on hers, the sweet smell of her hair and the gentle sigh that had come out of her mouth once her lips parted.

Her daydream was interrupted by the jiggle of the front doorknob and the boys suddenly bursting through the door, backpacks on and ready to tackle their aunt.

"Whoa, whoa, whoa," Mel said, breaking into a big smile and letting the boys climb on her, ignoring the strict no-shoes-in-the-house rule that her sister enforced.

Greg stood in the doorway and gave Mel a quick wave. "Nice to see you, Mel," Greg said. Mel gave him a hug as the boys moved to the kitchen to raid the snack cupboard. She had nothing against her sister's ex, but she had to admit she'd never really understood the two of them together. Chalk it up to young love. They were high school sweethearts, married by twenty-two and divorced by twenty-six.

At least he'd never cheated on Andie.

"They behave themselves?"

"Define behave," Greg said. "Tell Andie they each had two time-outs last night. Nothing serious, and we probably got them too wound up on sugar. But just so she knows."

Mel bid Greg farewell, then called the boys into the kitchen before they had the chance to get to their room. She wanted Andie to be the one to surprise them with their new beds. "How do you two feel about going on a mission with me?"

Their eyes lit up. "We love missions!" Matthew said. "Where to?"

"An incredible place. Where everything you need to get strong and survive is stored. We're on a mission to replenish our storage chests."

"Like in *Quest of Giladron*?" Ryan said.

"Uh, kind of," Mel said. "Except this place is called Fresh Mart. We're going to buy groceries. You two are going to help me make dinner so that your mom can have a break."

Ryan looked skeptical. "That doesn't sound like a very fun mission."

"How about this? After we make dinner, I'll take you two to the movies."

The boys cheered, and Mel smiled to herself. She knew this was an incredibly busy time for Andie, and their parents, regular snowbirds, had already headed down south for the fall and winter, so she'd be spending more time with the boys over the next while.

She got them buckled into Andie's car, double- and triple-checking their seat belts even though they'd reached the age that they could do it themselves. She didn't know how her sister did it, day in and day out, bearing such a huge responsibility, two perfect lives in her hands.

She and Breanne had talked about having kids, but it had always seemed like something so far away, that they would spend the beginning of their adult lives together, relishing in the perfection of their love. Kids would come later, she'd supposed. Back when she believed the world was a better place. Now? Mel struggled to think of how she would ever trust another person with herself, never mind an innocent child.

She listened to the boys prattle in the backseat the whole way to the store, bickering over who was a better soccer player in one minute, then trying to one-up each other with fart jokes the next. She was glad they had each other. Siblings, best friends.

She'd once known the feeling.

A scene from her teenage years played in her mind, the night that she and Lauren had packed up their camping gear, a pack of frozen hotdogs that would thaw as they hiked to their destination for the night and a bottle of Wild Turkey that Lauren had snuck from her parents' liquor cabinet, which still contained unfinished bottles from their wedding reception and therefore wouldn't be missed. It was the perfect August day, late enough in the summer that the bugs on the trails were mostly gone, and still warm enough that a light sleeping bag would do.

They'd traipsed through the forest trail, cracking jokes, singing at the top of their lungs, and then later, by the fire, talking about movies and university and everything else that was occupying their brains at the time.

After a couple of swigs of bourbon each, their conversation had approached the heart-to-heart territory, and Mel vividly remembered, despite the booze, how lucky she'd felt in the moment to have a best friend.

She'd loved Lauren like her own sister, and never could have imagined doing anything to hurt their friendship. So on the day when Lauren had come to her door, tears in her eyes, barely able to hold up her head, Mel realized that the feeling didn't go both ways. The depth of that betrayal would haunt her forever.

She looked at the boys in the rearview mirror, their innocent smiles lighting up their faces as they poked and teased one another. "Boys," Mel said, hoping they didn't notice the crack in her voice. Unbelievable. Almost three years later, and just thinking of Breanne and Lauren still got under her skin. "Promise me something?"

"What, Auntie Mel?" Matthew said.

"Promise me you'll always look out for each other. Siblings are special," she said.

The boys were quiet for a moment, and Mel wondered if they were too young to really wrap their heads around big life ideas like that. "Yeah," said Ryan seriously. "And smelly."

Suddenly the car was filled with laughter. "And smelly," Mel agreed, as she pulled into the parking lot at Fresh Mart. "Come on. Let's get some stuff to make tacos."

Chapter Ten

"So. One hundred and forty-one guests. Fifteen tables. Here's a rundown of people who don't play well together." Connie handed Georgia a list. A much longer list than Georgia had expected for such an easy-going small town where everyone seemed to coexist peacefully. What Connie had given her could potentially rival the last-minute guest list scramble for the *Vanity Fair* Oscars after-party, when the wrong winner for best picture had been announced and emotions were high.

"Got it," said Georgia. "Any good stories?" They were sitting at the table in Connie's sun-filled kitchen, with a coffee (complete with a shot of Baileys, at Connie's insistence) and a whole lot of drama to dissect.

"How long have you got?" Connie said, letting

out a hoot. "Stick around long enough next weekend and you'll see some fireworks. Every year, without fail. Goodness, sometimes I feel like I live in a soap opera. And you know who they come to for advice the next day? Me! I practically have to block off my calendar for the week after the event to deal with the fallout."

Georgia smiled, enjoying Connie's theatrics. Despite her complaints, the woman loved being in the thick of the drama. She'd be right at home in LA, in Georgia's industry.

It had been a hilarious two hours so far, discussing last-minute details for the fundraiser while Scamus lay on his back in the living room. Mel had been completely wrong about Georgia working with Connie. The two of them got on like wildfire and it barely felt like work.

"Now, you didn't hear it from me. But these two—" she pointed to two names on the list "—have been on and off again for years. And she promised her husband that they'd be off again permanently, but…it doesn't seem to have stuck. So, for the sake of everyone around them, let's put them at opposite sides of the room. Preferably with their backs to one another so that they're not making googly eyes at each other."

"Got it," Georgia said. "Keep the secret lovebirds flying in different skies."

Connie chortled. "Exactly. And Moira Kent, Carolyn Bello and Leena Armentrout—there's a recipe for disaster if they're seated together. Used to be thick as thieves, the three of them. Moira took Carolyn's side with a deciding vote on the community garden award. Then turned right around and copied Leena's design. They haven't spoken in over a year." She looked at Georgia's plate, which she'd piled with various shortbread cookies and a handful of Werther's Originals to go with their boozy coffees. "Now, you eat up! Your stomach's rumbling something fierce!"

Georgia gratefully plucked a shortbread from the plate and took a bite, the soft buttery crumble melting in her mouth. "You made these?" she asked. "They're incredible." Could she bring Connie home with her?

"Now, tell me," Connie said, with a conspiratorial whisper. "Who are we going to sit you with? A pretty thing like you, with no ring on her finger? I know this is a fundraiser, but the event can do double duty, can't it?"

"Oh, don't worry about me," Georgia said. She wondered what Connie would think if she knew that Georgia would be seating herself at Mel's table. And although she still had a lingering worry that getting too close to Mel was a step backward in her goal to depart Sunset County unscathed and distraction-free, she knew very well that putting herself anywhere else wasn't an option.

More than once since they'd kissed at the shelter she'd been tempted to text Mel, or call her, or find some way to be passing by her place when she knew she'd be taking Franny out for a walk. She was certain that the kiss had been just as mind-blowing for Mel as it was for her. Mel's hands gripping her waist like a vise. How she gently nibbled on Georgia's lower lip, making Georgia tremble like there was a jackhammer drilling the ground beside them. The want and need emanating from her like a burning heat wave. How the concern and care in Mel's eyes before she'd kissed Georgia had done a one-eighty to intense desire.

And then, she'd left. That part Georgia couldn't figure out, but she knew it wasn't for lack of chemistry. That had been a damn good kiss, and they both knew it.

Georgia would be finishing her time at the shelter, and the following Saturday night might be the last time she ever saw Mel. Was it so bad if she wanted to see if they could pick up where they'd left off? A dimly lit party was certainly more romantic than an animal shelter, so there was that too. And the fact that it might be their last night together made the idea safer. Georgia would be leaving regardless, so there'd be no chance for things to go further or for either of them to get hurt.

She looked up to see Connie peering at her over her reading glasses. "Where did you go, girl? That seating plan isn't going to make itself."

"On it!" Georgia said, hoping Connie wasn't some

kind of mind reader who was now fully aware of the fact that Georgia was mentally undressing her niece.

After another half hour of slotting guests into tables, Georgia wrapped a shortbread cookie in a napkin and tucked it in her purse, then slid her coat on. "Well, I'd say that was a productive meeting," she said. "If you think of anything else, just call me."

Connie stood up and stretched. "My dear, thanks to you, everything's hunk a-dee-doo at the zoo!" Then she paused, and a mischievous grin crept across her face. "Now, I wasn't going to say it, but I'm going to say it. Our Mel has been single for far too long. Do you think—"

"Connie, what did I tell you about meddling?" Seamus's voice called from the living room.

"What, you have nothing to say the whole time, and *now* you decide to chime in?" Connie yelled in his direction. "You'll be lucky if we don't seat you with Mayor Grimsby. Or that would be lucky for him, I guess." She looked back at Georgia and rolled her eyes.

"Your niece has been really helpful showing me around the shelter," Georgia said, diplomatically. No need to go any further than that.

"Well," Connie said, taking her elbow as she walked to the door. "We just hope she finds someone as nice as you one day. That other woman she was with…" She leaned in, whispering again. "Pretty girl. Skin like porcelain. But I always knew she was up to something. You know when people are *too* nice? They're always up to no good."

Georgia bid Connie farewell then called goodbye to Seamus.

Huh, she thought, as she walked down the path toward her car. *So Mel has an ex. An ex who wasn't exactly Miss Perfect.*

But who was she to judge? Wasn't the entire reason she was in Sunset County, the reason she'd met Mel Carter in the first place, because she wasn't exactly Miss Perfect herself?

It didn't matter. She'd be back home in a couple of weeks, and Mel Carter, Connie, Seamus, Hayley— they'd all be a distant memory, and Nina's cottage would be in the hands of perfect strangers. Georgia would make the big donation that would be her public atonement for her bad behavior. And then she'd be back on track to success.

Eye on the prize.

In a daze, Mel felt around on the bedside table for her phone. Who was calling at—what time was it? Three a.m.?

The bright screen displayed the emergency clinic phone routing number. It didn't happen often, but when it did, it was one of her client's pets requiring after-hours care. She blinked twice to clear her eyes, then tapped the screen to answer the call.

"Dr. Carter speaking," she said, trying to hide the grogginess in her voice.

"Dr. Carter, Officer Yu here," a female voice sounded from the line. *Officer Yu?* Why was she getting a call from the police?

Her heart started to race as she remembered the last time a police officer had called her. It was the call to let her know that Breanne was in the hospital, and she needed to get there as quickly as possible. She remembered her stomach bottoming out as she raced through the airport to get a cab, everything a blur, time speeding by and standing still at the same time.

"Hello? Are you there?"

"Yes, yeah, I'm here." She waited for the terrible news. Something had happened to Andie or one of the boys. Or Seamus. Or her parents, down south.

"Sorry to call you so early, but your number was listed on the shelter's voicemail. We responded to a domestic violence call earlier this morning and found what seemed to be some neglected dogs behind the residence. It's a large shed with a number of cages but we only found six back there. The dogs are…they're in bad shape. I would have waited until business hours to call you, but it looks like they need immediate medical attention."

Mel felt sick, both with the relief that her loved ones were safe, and at the idea of what she was about to walk into. After jotting down the address and changing quickly, she was walking out the front door, Franny whinnying at the unusual happenings as she locked up.

She stood on the driveway for a moment, considering. Six dogs. She'd need help. Seamus was still laid up, and her vet tech, Sandy, had just left the day before for a trip to Barbados with her boyfriend.

She paused before pulling her phone out of her pocket. She hadn't talked to Georgia since the day they'd kissed at the shelter, but it was no time for her pride to get in the way. She couldn't manage this on her own.

Georgia's voice was equally groggy on the other end when she picked up. "Mel? What's going on?"

"Sorry to wake you. But I'm going to need your help." Mel gave Georgia a quick rundown, asked her to meet her at the shelter and gave her instructions on how to prep one of the treatment rooms. The officer hadn't known what breed of dog they were dealing with, but she likened it to a small poodle, so luckily they weren't facing anything like a brood of Great Danes.

"Wait. I'll come with you," Georgia said. "Come pick me up. It won't take me long to get the room ready once we're there." Mel paused. It would be good to have another set of hands. The police were likely busy dealing with whatever had gone on in the house, so she'd probably be solo managing the dogs.

"Can you be ready in twenty?"

"I'll be waiting outside."

After grabbing some supplies from her clinic, Mel navigated the dark country roads toward Nina's cottage, feeling a sense of calm knowing that she was going into the situation with Georgia's assistance. The apprehension she'd been feeling before this moment had slightly dissipated.

When she pulled down the long lane leading to the cottage, she spotted Georgia out front. The headlights from her truck lit her up, and Mel's heart soared to see her. Dressed in jeans and what looked like one of her aunt's old work jackets, looking tired and without makeup, she was the most beautiful Mel had ever seen her.

She slid into the passenger seat. "Hey," Georgia said. "I'm glad you called."

Mel cleared her throat, unsure of what to say or do. Given that the last time they were together, they'd both seemed ready to rip each other's clothes off.

After making a three-point turn and getting back onto the road, she spoke. "Thank you for coming." She longed to reach over and grab Georgia's hand, but instead just glanced sideways to see her trying to stifle a yawn.

"Sorry," Georgia said. "I'm a deep sleeper. I'm surprised I woke up. Maybe I just sensed something was wrong."

Mel turned left on the main road that would take them to the address the officer had given her. They were about ten minutes away, and she knew Georgia needed to be prepped for what was coming. "Listen. I don't know what kind of shape these dogs are in, but I want you to know that it might be… It might be hard to see." She looked beside her to see Georgia nodding.

"I can take it," Georgia said.

"I know you can take it. It's just that it can be upsetting. And if these dogs were mistreated, there's no telling how they'll behave. I want you to stay back while I crate them. Okay?" Keeping Georgia safe was her first priority. The fact that she was willing to come in the middle of the night and help only left Mel without another reason to discount Georgia. The list was really thinning out.

"Okay," Georgia said.

"And there's always a chance they'll be too far gone. I'll make that call when we're back at the shelter. There's a possibility that one or more of them will need to be put down."

Georgia was quiet. "Who are these people?"

Mel seethed when she considered what they were about to walk into. "Damned if I know. And I'd better not see them. Or I'll get myself into some trouble. There's your other job. Make sure I don't do anything stupid."

Once again, Georgia was quiet, and once again, the only thing Mel wanted to do was reach over and touch her, squeeze her hand and reassure her that everything would be okay. As much as her presence was having a calming and reassuring effect on Mel, and even though Georgia was the most poised and competent woman she'd ever met, Mel felt a strong desire to protect her, to keep her safe.

She willed herself to focus on the road, to battle through the haze of the pre-dawn.

Several minutes later, she pulled the truck into a large vacant lot across the way from what she supposed was the house under investigation. Three police cars sat parked while two officers conferred at the side of the road.

The female officer, likely Officer Yu, waved her down. Mel slowed to a stop, the truck still idling, then rolled down her window. "Dr. Carter?" the officer asked. "Officer Yu. Thanks for coming so quickly."

"Of course," she said. "This is Georgia. She's my—" She paused. "She's helping me out."

"Thanks to you too, Georgia. We've got two officers in the house taking a statement from the wife. Husband's down at the station, waiting for a lawyer. If you want to follow me, I'll take you out back to the shed."

"Okay if we drive? I've got some stuff in the back that we'll need."

Officer Yu nodded and led them across the street, down the gravel pathway that led to the back of the property. Mel took in the house, which looked as though it hadn't seen a lick of paint in decades. The roof was spotted with the black marks of missing shingles, and plastic grocery bags taped to the inside of the windows obscured the interior of the home.

"Well, this looks bleak," Georgia said quietly.

"You're not kidding," Mel said. She pulled into where Officer Yu was pointing, a narrow spot beside a rusty silver Mercury Topaz sitting on deflated tires. She killed the ignition, then turned to face Georgia.

"You ready?" Georgia said, a look of determination in her still-tired eyes. Mel recognized that this was the look of Georgia going in strong, a face she likely donned on a regular basis while doing her job. Mel liked it.

"Let's go," Mel said. "Just remember what I said. We don't know what we're going into, so stay back, and I'll let you know the plan."

They exited the truck and followed Officer Yu to a shed about a hundred meters behind the house, almost as large and every bit as run down. Mel noticed that Georgia had taken her phone out of her pocket and was using the flashlight to illuminate the ground ahead of them.

"Here," Officer Yu said, handing Mel her flashlight. "I'll let you have a look in. They're in the back left corner."

"You can stay here," Mel said to Georgia. She didn't hear any noises coming from inside, which could be a good sign. Or maybe not.

She stepped into the shed, a foul smell greeting her as she entered. Wooden planks lined the floor, coated with trampled hay. She looked for a light switch, but when she flicked it, the room remained dark.

"You okay in there?" Georgia called.

"All good," Mel called back. At the sound of her voice, she heard a soft whimpering in the corner where Officer Yu had flagged. She approached the noise to find a small containment area lined with chicken wire. In the corner, her light flashed over what appeared to be a small black-and-white border collie, cowering away from the light. The dog had some patches of fur missing, and when Mel approached, she could see that it had overgrown nails.

She knelt down and whistled softly. The dog looked up at her. Mel's heart sank when she saw the dog's eyes, which were emanating a milky discharge. She wanted to call the dog over but knew it wouldn't come. It didn't appear to be aggressive, so luckily it wouldn't be too much of a challenge to get it in a cage.

She stood up and scanned the rest of the space with the flashlight, spotting two other dogs in the same pen, who were either sleeping, or too weak to move.

One other pen on the far wall housed the other three, who looked up at her wearily from the small sections of the space that they occupied. Six altogether, all in similar states of poor health. Their pens appeared to be full of urine and feces.

Mel felt a rage boil up in her. Not only had the

police responded to a domestic abuse call, but there was this as well? It was a good thing that the son-of-a-bitch criminal had already been brought down to the station. Even if no one pressed charges for domestic abuse, there sure as hell would be consequences for neglect of this degree. She took a deep breath. All her focus and efforts were needed to care for these dogs.

Outside the building, Georgia stood alone, waiting for her. "Officer Yu got called back to her team," she said. "She gave me her number and told us to keep her posted. They apparently already photographed the scene, so we can take them. They're alive, right?"

"Alive, but not in great shape," Mel said as she exited the shed. "Listen. I'm going to give them each a small amount of sedative, so we can get them in the crates without too much fuss." They walked back to the truck and Mel passed Georgia a pair of work gloves. "Can you set the crates out in a line right outside the entrance, with their doors open? I'll bring them out one by one. Once they're in, you can carry the crates to the back of the truck."

Georgia nodded and got right to work. Mel's heart, which had been breaking only moments ago, swelled as she watched Georgia take action. She might have waltzed into Sunset County in a pair of stilettos and an LA sheen, but Mel could tell that when push came to shove, Georgia O'Neill could get down to business in any situation. It was no wonder she was in the line of work she was in—she knew how to fix things. Make bad situations better. She thanked her lucky stars again that Georgia was there to help.

After approaching them slowly and carefully and administering a small dose of acepromazine between the gums and cheek of each dog, Mel gathered them and placed them in the crates. Georgia put each crate in the back of the truck, and Mel overheard her speaking gently to them as she carried them to safety.

Once the dogs were all in the back of the truck, carefully secured with straps, Mel did one more sweep of the shed to ensure no one was being left behind. The anger started to boil back up in her chest.

She removed her gloves and tossed them in the back of the truck. "Let's go."

Chapter Eleven

Nothing was more compelling or more attractive than seeing Mel at work. The sense of purpose, the care, the methodical problem-solving—despite the terrible situation they were in, it might have been the most attracted Georgia had ever been to someone.

Mel was quiet as she drove them toward the shelter. The dim light of early dawn had started to appear just above the tree line. Georgia had a slight headache, the kind that she usually experienced before an early flight after interrupted sleep.

"Are they going to be okay?" she asked.

Mel cleared her throat. "We'll see."

Georgia waited, but Mel was quiet again. She looked over to see her fingers gripping the steering wheel tightly, a steely expression in her eyes.

"Unforgivable," she muttered.

"What do you mean?"

"What I mean is that it's unforgivable. What those people did. You talk about how everyone deserves a second chance? This is why I don't believe it."

The silence in the car was deafening. In the past, Georgia would have disagreed. First, they didn't have any of the information or background. Her instinct was to look for a spin.

But what she'd seen? She had to agree with Mel. The treatment of those poor, defenseless animals was reprehensible. "You're right," Georgia said. "It's—it's so beyond wrong, I don't even know where to start."

Mel pulled the truck up to the shelter. "Are you sure you're ready for this? If it's too much, I understand. You can take my truck to get yourself home once we've unloaded the crates."

"No," Georgia said. "I want to help." There was no way she was going to leave before seeing the rescue through or leave Mel on her own to tackle such a challenging task. She knew it wasn't the first time Mel had dealt with something like this, but it was clear that she was affected. And Georgia wanted to be right there by her side.

They carried the crates in and lined them up outside the examination room. Georgia spread clean sheets of paper over the examination tables as Mel washed and cleaned each dog in another room.

"The tranquilizers will be in effect for another

hour or so," Mel said, when she returned to where Georgia was waiting. "That'll be enough time to really see what we're dealing with before they're fully aware of their surroundings."

Georgia looked at Mel as she continued to set up her space. Her cheeks were flushed, and her hair was tousled. Georgia's heart skipped a beat. She was filled with gratitude that Mel had thought to call her and was experiencing the same rush of adrenaline associated with problem-solving that she loved about her job, but this felt different. This felt like *more*. It felt important. And having this experience by Mel's side? She already felt closer to her in a way that she'd never felt close to anyone before.

"Alright. I'm going to bring the first one in," Mel said.

Georgia stood back and watched as Mel gently placed one of the dogs on the examination table. She couldn't stop herself from gasping, and immediately, tears stung her eyes as she took in the full picture that she hadn't been able to see in the dim light of the yard, through the slats of the crate.

The border collie looked to be in way worse shape than she'd thought. Would it even survive? It seemed impossible.

Mel looked up, and her determined expression softened. "Hey, hey, it's okay. I know it looks bad, but she's actually going to be alright." She looked at Georgia, eyes deep with concern. "Listen. I know you want to help, and I really appreciate it. You've already done a lot. I'm fine from here on out. You don't have to stay. Really."

Georgia approached the examination table. Leaving Mel was not an option. She willed the lump in her throat to disappear. "I'm okay. I want to stay. What can I do?"

Mel paused, her eyes searching Georgia's. "Alright. Pass me that ointment there. I'm going to put some antibiotic cream on these lesions."

Georgia passed her the tube of ointment, then observed for the next forty-five minutes as Mel treated each dog one at a time, calmly and competently applying ointments and eye drops and administering injections. She directed Georgia to clean and disinfect their crates and line each one with a clean blanket. The dogs would stay in their crates until they were fully awake, at which point they would take each one out and reassure them that they were safe.

"They're docile, which is good," Mel said. "But it'll take them a long time to trust humans again. So don't expect them to warm up to us anytime soon. Or ever, maybe."

"So what happens with them, then?" Georgia asked. "Like, when they get better? Will anyone ever want to adopt a pet that doesn't want to be around people?"

"They have a much better chance than an aggressive dog, which many abused animals become. Oftentimes those ones need to get put down. My instinct is that these pups will find homes, eventually. They'll just need somewhere to heal for a while first."

The idea of the weak, injured dogs someday being welcomed into safe and loving homes filled Georgia with relief. And that they'd get better under the warm, caring roof of the Sunset County Animal Shelter was icing on the cake. They'd be better within a month, hopefully.

A month. By that time, Georgia would have been home for weeks, and everything that had happened would be water under the bridge. That's the way it was in Hollywood. Your mistakes were broadcast and scrutinized in an unimaginable way, until there was another distraction and you became yesterday's news. In a month, Georgia would be back on track, far away from Sunset County. It struck her suddenly that she would never see the dogs get better, and she wouldn't be there for the day when their loving new families came to pick them up and take them home to their new lives.

Tears pricked her eyes again, which were heavy with exhaustion. Georgia checked her watch. It was coming on 6 a.m.

"Are you okay here for a few minutes?" she asked Mel. "I'm just going to run and grab a coffee down the street."

Mel looked up briefly and nodded, and in the short moment that she held Georgia's gaze in hers, Georgia felt like she was looking at her in a whole different way.

The sun was starting to appear over the treetops, and a white mist was heavy near the ground. It was going to be a beautiful day. Not that Georgia would see much of it. She yawned, thinking of what it would feel like to crawl back into the bed she'd vacated hours earlier.

Anna was just putting out the wooden sign advertising the specials outside of the shop when Georgia approached the entrance.

"This is an early one for you," she called when she looked up and saw Georgia. "Especially on a Sunday!"

"You're not kidding," Georgia said, stifling a yawn. She filled Anna in on the events of the morning.

"That's just sick," Anna said as Georgia followed her inside. It was the only time Georgia had been in the shop without it being filled to the brim with customers, but somehow, like everything else in Sunset County, it still maintained the feeling of home.

Anna shook her head. "Latté?" she asked.

"Yes. And a chamomile tea. Bag out," she said. How long had it been since she'd known another person's beverage order?

Anna passed her the two drinks and waved away Georgia's debit card. "On the house," she said. "What you two did deserves some recognition, so take that as a small thank-you."

"You don't have to—"

"I insist. That's what they call everyday heroism."

Georgia grinned. "Well, that might be a bit much. But thank you. I'm sure Mel will appreciate it too."

On the walk back to the shelter, Georgia took a small sip of her latté. Maybe it was the wild night they'd had, or the warm feeling she had inside from being told she'd done something good, but it was the best damn latté she'd ever had.

Georgia let herself back into the shelter. "Mel?" she called, but was met with only the sound of the reception computer's fan. At the end of the hallway, she noticed the door to the outdoor area ajar and as she approached, she heard Mel's voice coming from outside. Was she talking to herself? She took a few steps down the hallway and paused outside the doorway.

"Six. Yeah. One looks pretty bruised in the abdomen, and two of them have several missing teeth. But they're all cleaned up, and I gave them a bit more acepromazine." She was on the phone, Georgia guessed, with Seamus. She was quiet while listening to the other end. "No, no, don't worry about coming in. I've got it covered. Georgia came with me." She was quiet again, and Georgia stood silently, holding her breath. "Yeah. She really is. It's— She's been—" She hesitated, and Georgia suddenly felt wrong for eavesdropping on a private conversation, but she hung on, desperate to know what Mel thought about her. "She's surprised me in every way."

Georgia leaned against the doorframe, Mel's words filling her with warmth. She knew exactly what Mel had thought of her the day she'd first come to the shelter, and knowing her perspective had changed, now that she actually knew her, meant everything.

She listened as Mel signed off, then waited a moment before clearing her throat, and pushing open the back door. She found Mel leaning against the picnic table, a faraway look in her eyes. She stood up straight when Georgia walked out, as though she'd caught her in the act of something she shouldn't have been doing.

"Hey," Georgia said, looking around. "How are things here?"

"All good," Mel said. "They're all in their crates. I just talked to my uncle. Seems like we're done for now."

The sun had finally appeared above the tree line, casting long shadows over the pens. The animals were quiet, and with no wind, the back area was coated with a blanket of serenity.

Georgia passed Mel the peppermint tea. "Here. I still don't know how you don't drink caffeinated beverages but thought you might want something warm."

Mel had a funny look in her eyes. She took a deep breath as though she was about to say something, then stopped. She reached for the tea, then placed it behind her on the picnic table, returning her hand to Georgia's, grasping it.

Georgia's heart started to speed up, the electricity from Mel's touch doing more to jolt her awake than any coffee ever could.

"Thank you," Mel said, her voice slightly lower than usual, awakening something deep in Georgia.

"It's—it was Anna's treat," she breathed, wanting that same hand that held hers everywhere on her, all at once.

"Not for that. For everything you've done." Mel's eyes fixed on hers intently, causing Georgia's heart to race double time.

"I didn't—" Georgia stopped when Mel's hand reached up, her finger touching Georgia's lips, silencing her.

"And then this morning. And everything over the past few weeks. You weren't kidding when you said you're good at turning around bad situations."

Georgia could only nod, and had to remind herself to breathe. Only the soft chirping of the morning sparrows filled the silence. She listened intently, every word coming out of Mel's perfect lips washing over her, telling her everything she needed to hear after being knocked so far down. But Mel was done talking.

Her other arm slid around Georgia's waist, pulling them closer together, but Georgia was already moving that way of her own accord.

With her eyes closed, all of Georgia's focus was on the warmth emanating from Mel's lips as they approached hers. *Kiss me. For goodness' sake, kiss me.* Never in her life had she felt such an intense thirst of anticipation, as though she'd crossed a desert, *two* deserts, and Mel was holding back the cold water she so desperately needed.

Most people saw a kiss as a precursor to more exciting things. But whoever was lucky enough to kiss Mel Carter? That idea might be upended. The woman knew how to make the most instinctual of human touches into a full-blown fantasy.

"You're an incredible woman, Georgia O'Neill," Mel murmured, and then her lips were on Georgia's, finally, perfectly and hungrily. Georgia moaned gently, pressing her body into Mel's solid frame. "And you're an unbelievable kisser."

"You are," Georgia whispered. Their tongues met again gently before Mel separated her lips from Georgia's and started to kiss the sensitive skin on the side of her neck. Her warm breath caused an involuntary gasp, and an electric shiver made Georgia quake, her knees almost buckling out from under her. Up the side of her face, across her chin, Mel left a trail of soft but hungry kisses, until her lips met Georgia's once again, like two superpowered magnets.

She was addicted to kissing Mel Carter. The fact that there was more to look forward to beyond this, when they finally found themselves somewhere more appropriate than the hallway of the shelter or an animal enclosure, was the most exciting icing on the cake of all time.

When their lips finally separated, Georgia kept her eyes closed and moved her cheek next to Mel's, her breath tickling the hair tucked behind her ear.

"You should stay for a while. In town," Mel said.

Georgia almost couldn't bring herself to say it. "The cottage is going live on the market," she said, the truth only slightly tempering the vibration from the kiss. "Today." She took a deep breath, pulled back and studied Mel's face, still breathing deeply. "We'll be taking bids next Monday. I'm going home next week. As long as I get good news from my bosses."

Mel's expression didn't so much as harden as it did neutralize. What was she thinking? Feeling? It was impossible to know, but it was as though in a moment she'd gone from sensitive and vulnerable to robotic and unfeeling.

"So, you're really leaving."

Georgia nodded. But the kiss was perfect, and every part of her wanted more. She hesitated, and the look in Mel's eyes changed.

The early-morning air was silent. Mel ran her fingers through her hair. "Come on," Mel said. "I'll drive you home." The spell was broken.

"What about the dogs?" Georgia asked, trying to fill in the silence.

"They'll be down for another hour or so. I'll have a quick nap, then come back and spend some time with them."

Georgia tried to make conversation on the way back to Nina's place, but she was exhausted, and the vibrations between them were tempered by the futility of their situation. Her lips buzzed, still feeling Mel's lips on hers, and in spite of her fatigue, her body ached to be touched by her.

"Get some sleep," Mel said as she pulled up in front of the cottage. "I'll call you later." She reached over and kissed Georgia's head with a level of care that Georgia readily absorbed. She wasn't making things any easier.

She watched as Mel drove away, then went back inside the cottage, which had been perfectly staged, the remaining boxes moved out to the shed to be picked up by Goodwill.

She sank into the corduroy couch, mind swirling with the events of the past several hours. When she unlocked her phone, a notification showed a message from Hayley.

Listing's live! it read, with some emojis of happy faces, money, crossed fingers and a bottle of champagne.

She looked around the cottage. It was just about time to say goodbye.

Chapter Twelve

Over the next week, Georgia distracted herself by putting in extra hours at the shelter while the cottage was available for showings. Mel stopped by here and there to check on the animals, and to suggest some work for Georgia to do, but Georgia was mostly on her own as Mel caught up with the backlog of appointments at her clinic. Georgia also suspected that Mel might be keeping her distance on purpose.

In any event, the week was flying by, and Georgia was enjoying the work more by the day and appreciating her remaining time with the animals. She'd posted a few more profiles to the shelter's Instagram page, and there had been a steady stream of interested people coming through to meet the animals in person.

Georgia was tired yet satisfied. She was also grateful to be out of Nina's place while the showings were taking place.

On Friday morning, the day of her last shift, Mel arrived at the shelter with a Rise and Grind latté for her.

Georgia grinned from her spot at the reception desk as she accepted the takeout cup from Mel. "Thank you," she said. "I'm going to miss these."

Mel leaned against the front counter, fixing Georgia with her deep brown stare. "What, they don't have lattés in Hollywood? Maybe you'll wean yourself off the caffeine a bit."

Georgia grinned. "Not as good as these ones." She took a sip. "Mmm. Amazing. Thank you again." She noticed Mel wasn't taking off her coat. "Leaving already?"

"I have back-to-back appointments today. But I'll be back later this afternoon. Do you have time to come on a house call with me? There's something I want to show you."

"What is it?" This was new. And Mel had been avoiding her all week. But her expression was playful. Georgia was dying to know what was in store.

"You'll have to see."

"So mysterious. Okay. Am I dressed appropriately?"

Mel raised an eyebrow, the amused expression spreading across her face. "You haven't been dressed appropriately since the moment you walked through that door."

Georgia laughed. "Whatever." She looked down at her Rag & Bone light-wash jeans and her cream-colored Theory cardigan. "I'd call this casual yet professional."

"Hey, I'm not complaining. I'll be back around three-thirty. See you soon." She gave Georgia a quick wave before sliding on her aviator sunglasses.

"See you," Georgia said. She sat back in her chair, taking another long sip of her latté. Damn. Mel looked beyond sexy in sunglasses. In anything, really.

The rest of the day flew by as Georgia did one last run-through of her usual tasks, and then spent a few minutes saying goodbye to each of the animals in the shelter. She also made sure to snap a good photo of each of them.

Georgia made the rounds, starting with the border collies, who were making encouraging progress. She even tapped on Slinky's tank to say goodbye. Despite Mel's protestations that they couldn't take in any new animals, the Harris family had dropped off four of the kittens they hadn't managed to find families for and she saved the little orange-and-white kitten for last. When she lifted him out of the enclosure, the kitten purred against her chest. "What should we call you?" Georgia whispered. "Pumpkin? Creamsicle?" She held the little cat out and inspected him. "No. You need something more special. As perfect as you are. I'll give it a think."

The shelter's front door chimed, and Georgia gave

the kitten a big kiss. "You'll find a family," she said, feeling the little cat's soft fur against her cheek. "And they'll be so lucky to have you."

She heard Mel call her name from the front entrance, gave the little kitten one last nuzzle and deposited him back in his pen with his three other siblings.

"Now, don't get all sentimental," she said to herself, but she still had to take a deep breath in and steady her shoulders before joining Mel at reception. She stood for a moment in the doorway before flicking off the light switch, natural light from the window replacing the fluorescent lights overhead.

"You ready?" Mel asked, standing at the front entrance with her keys and a small cardboard box.

"Are you going to tell me where we're going?"

"You'll find out when we get there. Let's go."

Georgia got in her car and followed Mel's truck away from Main Street, out to one of the county highways. About fifteen minutes later, Mel signaled into a long gravel driveway that led to a big blue barn sitting next to a farmhouse, with acres of cornfields behind it. Behind the rows of golden, dried-out cornstalks was a thick forested area.

She parked her car behind Mel's truck, then got out of the car and surveyed her surroundings. The late-fall air was crisp and cool, and as though Mel was reading her mind, she passed Georgia a pair of mittens. "Here," she said. "I figured you wouldn't have any."

Georgia warmed at the small kindness and pulled the wool mittens on. It was a bit confusing, though. One minute, Mel was breaking away from the most perfect kiss of all time and seemingly avoiding Georgia. Then, she was bringing her thoughtful gifts and taking her on a mysterious outing? What the heck was going on? "So, what are we doing here?"

"Come on," Mel said. She led Georgia to the entrance of the barn, where they were greeted by a tall, sturdy man, maybe in his early thirties, wearing work clothes and a wide smile.

"Hey, Doc," he said. He stuck his fist out, and Mel returned the bump. "Thanks for coming by."

"Anytime," Mel said. She passed him the box she'd had with her at the shelter. "Knox, this is Georgia. She's been helping us at the shelter the last few weeks." Georgia noted the hint of pride in her voice.

She got a fist bump from Knox too. "Nice to meet you, Knox." She liked him right away. He had that kind of warm presence that made people feel comfortable and welcomed, like he didn't have a bad bone in his body and you could rely on him to come pick you up in the middle of the night if you had a flat tire. Georgia wondered if he'd known Nina; they seemed like two peas in a pod in that regard.

"So, Georgia, I hear you like horses," he said. "You've come to the right place."

"I love horses," Georgia said. She looked at Mel and opened her mouth wide. "Stop. Did you bring me here to see horses? Amazing!" She turned back to Knox. "She's not just a great vet. She's a very thoughtful boss. I only mentioned that, what, one time?"

Mel bit her lip, as though she was trying to hold back a huge grin. "I saw how you connected with Taffy. And we're going to do more than just see the horses here."

Georgia all but squealed with excitement. "This is amazing!" No one, aside from Nina, had ever done something like this for her. A moment of pure fun. Nothing to add to her résumé. Just the thrill of a new experience, for experience's sake.

Knox held up the box. "You want to do this now, Doc, or after our outing?"

"We'll do it after," Mel said. "We drove separately, and Georgia probably has stuff to do tonight." She looked at Georgia. "Vaccinations. For one of the horses."

"Shall we, then?" Knox motioned to the stable's entrance.

The interior of the barn was brightly lit, with the earthy but not unpleasant smell of dusty hay. Each side of the structure was lined with ten stalls. As they walked down the length of the barn, Georgia oohed and aahed at the stately, powerful animals, some of whom sniffed and nickered as she passed. Knox stopped at the second to last stall. "I picked this one out for you," he said, pointing at a chestnut mare with a sturdy leather saddle on her back. "Her name's Mindy."

"It's love at first sight," Georgia said, approaching the stall and marveling at Mindy's stately frame and probing, gentle eyes. "Am I really going to ride her?"

"Only if you want to," Mel said. "Knox offered to take us through the forest trail. It's about forty minutes down and back."

Knox got Georgia outfitted in a helmet and a pair of riding boots and showed her how to lead Mindy by her reins out to the yard. He and Mel followed suit with two other horses, a dark brown Clydesdale named Jasper and a black Friesian named Klaus.

"How do I get all the way up there?" Georgia asked, eyeing Mindy's height. "Is there a stool or something?"

"Come on over to the left side," Knox said. "Get the ball of your foot right in here," he said, pointing to the stirrup. "Hold the reins in your left hand while you stand up. And then just swing your right leg over. Careful not to kick her."

Georgia prayed she wouldn't miss the mark and end up on her back in the dirt. But she was surprised by how easy it was to follow Knox's directions, and within seconds she'd safely mounted Mindy, who made it easy on her by staying completely still.

"Look at you!" Mel said, beaming at her from a few feet down. "No big deal!"

Georgia sat up straight on the horse, loving the

feeling of being on top of the majestic being. "This is already the best," she said, looking over to watch as Mel hopped up on her saddle as though it was the most natural thing in the world.

Knox led them out of the barn and into the yard, patiently explaining to Georgia how to sit relaxed in the saddle while they were riding, how to get Mindy to slow down with a simple "Whoa," and how to get her to walk by giving her a gentle squeeze with her legs.

Knox took the lead, followed by Georgia, with Mel at the rear.

"Seems like you're a natural," Mel said. Georgia turned around to look at her and found her grinning ear to ear. Had she ever seen such excitement in Mel's eyes? Had Mel changed her mind about maintaining a wall between them?

The forest trail was covered with the fallen leaves of the sugar maples and red oaks, which were now mostly bare, and the path they followed was lined with pussy willows and grasses all dried up from a hot summer.

Georgia marveled at how sure-footed the horses were, even when navigating around fallen branches and over the rocky base of a small trickling creek.

"Let me take your picture," Mel said, when Knox was a bit farther ahead and out of earshot.

"Whoa," Georgia said, and just like that, Mindy slowed to a stop as Mel came up beside them.

"You look really great." Mel slid her phone from

a pocket in the chest of her jacket, and it took no effort for Georgia to break into a wide smile.

"Can you get one with both of us in it?" Georgia said, fully expecting Mel to say no or roll her eyes at the idea of ending up on Georgia's social media.

"Sure thing," Mel said. She held the phone out in front of her to capture them both in a selfie.

"Make sure you send me those," Georgia said. It was a moment she always wanted to remember. This trip had been full of surprises, most of all the woman riding beside her.

Long streaks of late-afternoon sun combed through the forest and lit Mel and her horse up in a golden glow. Aside from the clomping of the horses' hooves through the leaves, the quiet of the forest was only punctuated every now and then by a bird's call. It was the most peaceful place Georgia had ever been.

When they caught up to Knox, he pointed out an intricately carved wooden bear to the side of the path, which appeared to be standing sentinel and protecting the forest behind it.

"My grandfather made that when we were kids," he said. "He put it there to mark the edge of the property."

"It's beautiful," Georgia said. "And what a huge piece of land."

"Might be selling some of it soon, actually," Knox said. "We don't need it all, and the financial cushion would help us. There's a company looking to build a country retreat, all eco-friendly and respectful of the history of the land and its First Peoples. The area needs it. It's almost impossible to book a room anywhere around here in the peak season. So, we're in talks."

"I'd come back in a heartbeat," Georgia said. "It's so serene here." She hadn't pictured herself ever coming back to Sunset County after Nina's estate was settled. Now, she felt a connection and a draw to the place that her aunt must have experienced. The idea that she could come back made it a bit easier to stomach leaving so soon.

She glanced over at Mel, who was looking at her intently.

"Glad to hear it," Mel said. She cleared her throat. "Shall we make our way back?"

"You got it, Doc," Knox said.

The ride back was quiet, and Georgia did her best to soak in the peace of the forest, which was competing with the current of excitement rippling through her as she watched Mel ride ahead of her, her strong body absorbing the bumpy ride and looking totally at home and at ease with her horse.

Georgia could have gladly done another loop, but she didn't want to overstay her welcome. "That was awesome. I really loved it," Georgia said, as Knox helped her dismount Mindy. "And thank you, Mindy." Georgia ran her hand over Mindy's soft coat. "You're a beauty. I hope you get lots of carrots."

"Oh, she will," Knox said. He stuck out his hand to shake Georgia's. "Great to meet you. Come on by anytime."

Mel walked Georgia to her car while Knox brought the horses back to their stalls. "So, did it live up to your expectations?" she asked. Her eyes danced with pleasure and Georgia knew it mattered to Mel that her idea for an excursion had panned out.

"Exceeded. I'm hooked." She suddenly wished they hadn't taken separate cars, so she'd have an excuse to hang around longer. "Thank you for arranging this. It was perfect." She opened the door to her car, then turned to Mel, who was still beaming a smile that was spread all over her face. "Be my date," Georgia blurted out. "To the fundraiser tomorrow." A few weeks in a small town and she'd already lost her razor-sharp judgment. It was high time she got home. But as she gazed at Mel's stunning chocolate brown eyes, she felt herself unwinding. How much harm could one night out do? "I mean, I'll have to meet you there. Connie will need my help before the party starts. But it would be fun. To be there together." Since when was she a babbler? She bit her lip to keep her mouth shut.

"Sounds great," Mel said. Her cheeks were flushed with pink and her wavy hair had a windswept look to it, and Georgia felt herself totally under Mel's spell. She was surprised by how easily Mel had accepted her invitation, and that she'd gone out of her way to do something so nice for Georgia. "Get home safely, okay?"

As much as she longed to stay by Mel's side, Georgia got into her car. Mel waited until she was safely inside, then closed the door and knocked twice on the roof. Georgia waved goodbye to Mel and navigated her car back to the road. *Home.*

For a flash, Georgia imagined what it would be like to call Sunset County home. A quiet life. With nature and community and space to breathe. She'd never understood the appeal until now.

But her life, her work, everything she considered home was thousands of miles away. This romanticizing of small-town life would fade as soon as she touched down at LAX, she was sure of it. Sunset County would be a memory in the rearview mirror. So why did she already miss it?

The sky was a blaze of tangerine and saffron as the early November sun was dipping behind the trees. Mel watched Georgia's Audi disappear down the county highway before returning to the barn, where she found Knox scrubbing feed buckets in a deep metal sink.

"What's that song?" asked Knox as she approached. Mel hadn't even realized she was whistling. She felt light as air. Could the afternoon have been more perfect? The golden light of fall pouring over the forest, the gentle whinny of the horses. The look in Georgia's eyes when Mel told her they were going riding. The way Georgia adorably stumbled over words while asking Mel to be her date to the fundraiser.

Two weeks earlier she would never have believed it. A date? But now, why not? Maybe it was time she had a great night with a beautiful woman. No strings attached. Georgia was leaving, but there were other beautiful women, right? This could be the sign she had to get back out there.

"Just something stuck in my head," Mel said. "Can I give you a hand?"

"Nah, all set," Knox said. He placed the bucket he was cleaning on the ground and wiped his hands on his jeans. "Georgia seems great. Never seen you all dreamy-eyed like that, Doc."

Mel gave him a look. "I don't know what you're talking about." But he was right. Being with Georgia had left her in a dreamlike state, and she'd be kidding herself if she thought another woman could slide in and easily take Georgia's place.

"Like this," Knox said, batting his lashes and clasping his hands together dramatically across his chest.

"What, like how you always look at my sister?" Mel said, grinning. "Don't think I've never noticed." Knox and Andie had been friends since middle school, when she'd asked him to pretend to be her boyfriend on the playground to make another schoolmate jealous. Knox hadn't minded playing the role, and Mel had long suspected that there might have been some wishful thinking on his part from that moment on.

Knox laughed, but his face went beet red. "No way. Trust me. I know she's too good for me."

Mel smiled. She knew their friendship was important to Andie; otherwise, he'd be on the short list of guys she'd approve for her sister to date. She picked up the vaccine kit she'd brought with her. "Alright, are we doing this?"

While Mel prepared the boosters for the one-year-old filly she'd come to attend to, Knox pulled up a chair, put his feet up on a dusty wooden barrel and started whittling a small piece of wood with a pocketknife.

"So, when's your property getting listed?" Mel asked. "Any chance this fancy retreat would want to showcase a selection of adorable, orphaned animals?" She smoothed the skin of the filly's neck she'd just swabbed with an alcohol wipe. Pinching the skin gently, she administered the dose in one efficient action, then repeated the action twice more with the other vaccines before gathering and tossing the materials into the trash bin.

"You know I'll take in that little brown pony if there are no takers. And as for the sale, we're just waiting for the county office to confirm the property lines. Then we'll see what the company has to offer. By the sounds of it, they'll be looking to break ground by next fall."

"That's exciting."

"Indeed." He paused, then grinned. "Maybe Georgia will come back to visit."

Mel zipped up her coat and shot him a look. "Maybe you'll mind your own business."

Knox tossed her the small piece of wood he'd been carving. She caught it and examined the figure in her hand, which was in the shape of a horseshoe. "You're not as poker-faced as you might think, Doc. Just sayin'."

"Uh huh," Mel said, smiling. She said goodbye to Knox and returned to her truck, where she tucked the small wooden carving in the pocket of the driver's side visor. *A little luck.* She'd never believed in it. Were things finally starting to go her way?

She honked twice as she pulled away from the barn, and it wasn't until she got back onto the county highway when she realized that the radio was off, and the light notes of music in the truck were once again coming from her own mouth.

Chapter Thirteen

On Saturday morning, Georgia got up early, intent on enjoying her last few days in the area. Sunset County no longer seemed dead and boring, like it had when she'd arrived. It just existed on its own wavelength, and it was like Georgia had finally synced with the new frequency.

After a coffee and croissant at Rise and Grind, she spent some time poking around the small shops on Main Street, where she found some gorgeous dress options for the gala at a women's clothing shop called Wish. If she didn't know better, they could have been mistaken for designer pieces.

She browsed the bookshop, went for a long walk along the lakeside trail, then stopped for lunch at The Peony, where she leafed through her new Louise Penny mystery novel and enjoyed a plump Reuben sandwich with a side salad of peppery arugula and goat cheese.

After that, it was time to return to Nina's cottage to prepare for the gala.

In Georgia's experience, if there was one thing that was a reliably good time, it was getting ready for an event. She had perfected her routine over the years, and while tonight's event would be a less glitzy affair than she was used to preparing for, she would be following the same steps: early-afternoon nap with under-eye patches on. A long, luxurious shower, followed by a light meal. And then her favorite part: an upbeat playlist blaring out of her Bluetooth speaker and a glass of cava with her hair and makeup team. Unfortunately they wouldn't be on hand for this evening, but Georgia had learned enough over the years to pull together a great look on her own.

She spilled the contents of her cosmetics bag across the counter, humming along with the "top hits of 2014"—a throwback, but a particularly good year from that decade.

Georgia examined her face in the mirror prior to applying any makeup. She had to admit, her time in Sunset County had done her good. Gone were the under-eye shadows from her long working hours. Eating a bit more (how many of those Rise and Grind croissants had she put away?) had also filled in her face a bit—maybe she had been a bit gaunt as of late.

Certainly around the time of Nina's death and her meltdown she'd barely eaten for a good week and a half, which hadn't helped. Now, she looked refreshed. Alive. Dare she say *happy*?

With a Sia track playing in the background, she dabbed some foundation on a makeup sponge, then paused and inspected her reflection a little more closely. A thought occurred to her. Something that mere weeks ago would have been an unimaginable idea.

Maybe she'd go to the fundraiser without makeup. She looked good, right? Why cover up the best she'd looked in a long time? Even the idea of it felt a bit defiant, a bit of a thrill. She'd worn at least mascara every day since the seventh grade, when she'd stolen a tube from her mother's bag of cosmetics, applying it on the school bus (waiting for the stretches of roads that she knew to be relatively bump-free) and then using her fingertips to crumble it off on the way home so her parents didn't know. And recently? There was no way she would have faced down a Hollywood soiree without the armor of her foundation or lipstick, likely ducking into the bathroom a few times during the evening to reapply some powder or check that her eyeliner hadn't smudged. The idea of going barefaced was slightly terrifying. But liberating.

She checked her watch. One hour until departure. What to do with the extra time that had been reserved for painting her face? She thought of how much more she could accomplish with an extra thirty minutes in her day, every day. Maybe she was onto something.

A little voice sounded in her mind, reminding her what Connie had said about Mel's ex. *Pretty girl. Skin like porcelain.* Could she ever be worthy of that description?

Sparkling wine in hand, Georgia walked around the cottage, the little place that had really started to feel like home. As much as she was looking forward to being back in LA and feeling the sun on her face, she would miss Nina's cottage, which had enveloped her in a giant bear hug since the moment she'd arrived in Sunset County.

On the wall in the hallway leading to the kitchen, Georgia noticed a little cross-stitch of a blue jay that she'd neglected to pack. She examined the back, and recognized Nina's steady signature on the wooden frame.

What couldn't you do? Georgia thought as she returned to the dining room. She placed it on top of the box of keepsakes she would be taking home with her, right next to the sleeve of Nina's diaries, which she'd managed to avoid reading all week. Now, having had a few sips of her drink and with an extra bit of time on her hands, she figured it wouldn't hurt to skim through one of the books, just to see what had been on Nina's mind. For some reason, it didn't feel like as much of an invasion of privacy as she'd initially thought it might; after all, everyone knew that leaving a diary lying around was practically asking for someone to read it.

Sitting back on the couch, she flipped to the first page, which was dated February 1, almost five years earlier. She tried to remember what she knew about Nina's life at that point. She'd just retired from her job at the school the previous summer, and Georgia remembered that September, and her visiting LA, marveling at how decadent (and inexpensive!) it was to travel while school was in session. Nina had rented a room at the Petit Ermitage hotel in West Hollywood, since Georgia had still been living in her small one-bedroom apartment. They'd had eggs Benedict and Bloody Marys for brunch on the hotel rooftop, then spent the day lounging by the pool. They'd munched on pretzels and read old paperbacks that Nina had packed, dog-earing their pages every now and then to pause and chat, Nina indulging Georgia by listening to every last detail about her work and her life. Had Georgia asked her aunt any questions, or showed even a passing interest in her aunt's life? She wasn't sure.

She read through the first entry of Nina's familiar slanted script, which was an account of an interaction Nina had with a friend earlier that day. A fight, it seemed. *As usual, nothing I said made it past his stubborn skull*, Nina had written. *But, just as expected, he knocked on the door at six-thirty. Half an*

*hour before dinner. Good thing I know him as well as
I do, otherwise I'd have had to share my pork chop.*

Georgia laughed to herself, totally able to hear the
words as though Nina was in the room with her. She'd
been something of a mind reader, and could always
predict someone's actions in an eerily prescient way.
You're going to be a huge success, Nina had told her
that day at the rooftop pool, after a couple of late-
afternoon mezcal margaritas, when the sun was starting to dip. *And then one day you'll give it all up when
you find what you really love.*

Ha, Georgia had responded, tossing a pretzel at her
aunt. *You're half right. I'm going to be a huge success.
And* that's *going to make me happy.*

Then, Nina smiled that same smile that Georgia
knew meant *we'll see*.

Georgia read on, and noticed that the same friend
appeared in almost every entry. Jon, his name was.
And it didn't take more than four entries for Georgia
to put together the pieces—that Jon was more than
just a friend. In fact, the entry dated March 19 cleared
up any doubt in Georgia's mind. She snapped the
diary shut, knowing that she had crossed a privacy
line. And that Nina had definitely had what seemed
like a great sex life.

So why had Georgia never heard of this Jon? Or
known that Nina had been in love?

Her calendar alarm vibrated in her pocket, noti-
fying her of the night's event, and Georgia gasped

when she noticed the time. She had only minutes to get out the door if she wanted to be there for when Connie had requested her. She dialed the number for the cab company she'd found on a card in Nina's junk drawer (no Uber? Really?) and ordered a car. "ASAP!" Georgia said to the dispatcher.

She shed her pajama pants and sweatshirt and after trying on a couple of the dresses she'd bought that afternoon, she slid the chartreuse silk slip dress over her shoulders. She fastened Nina's gold sand dollar necklace around her neck, smoothed her hair, then slid her feet into a pair of black stilettos.

There was no full-length mirror in the cottage, but the dress itself was beautiful, so Georgia figured she looked good enough. She was ready to go. And without makeup!

"You're late!" exclaimed Connie, who was barefoot, her face flushed as she struggled with the easel for the seating arrangement.

"Here, let me give you a hand with that," Georgia said, knowing it wouldn't be useful or productive to point out that she was a mere four minutes past the time she was asked to arrive, and there was still a good hour and a half before the guests were due to get there. She steadied the easel, placed the large cardboard chart on it and stood back to observe. "How many fireworks do you think we're about to set off?" she asked Connie. "And look at you! Royal blue is definitely your color." Connie might have been annoyed at Georgia's "late" arrival, but Georgia knew how to get back on the woman's good side.

"I wore this for Mel's graduation party when she finished vet school. Can you believe it still fits?"

"You look absolutely fabulous," Georgia said. "Hot AF. Now. What else needs doing?"

Connie did a little curtsy, then rattled off a list of tasks, and Georgia busied herself finalizing the last-minute details, all the while trying to keep from looking at the entrance to the room every ten seconds.

An hour later, after securing a couple of lists that had come loose with tape, Georgia stood back and surveyed the seating chart again. "I see you got everyone's favorite party-planning task," a voice said from behind her. That sultry, sexy voice that had just run its fingers through her hair and traced them over the soft skin of her neck.

Georgia's stomach did a somersault as she took in the sight of Mel in a perfectly cut navy suit, crisp baby blue dress shirt unbuttoned one button, her hair falling in soft waves, her eyes even more intense than usual.

Eyes that were currently burning with desire as Georgia felt them trace every inch of her body, then settle back on her face.

Georgia suppressed an overwhelming desire to touch Mel. To have Mel touch her. To fast-forward to the part of the evening when it would be appropriate to whisper something deliciously cheeky in her ear, to suggest they move on to somewhere more private. Where Mel could touch her in all the ways she wanted, *needed*, to be touched. Georgia wanted all of Mel, from her arresting presence and exquisite face, to everything she'd come to know about her in the last several weeks. Her serious nature. Her calm competence. The undercurrent of nurturing that showed itself when she was so focused and intent on her work. Georgia wanted to be Mel's work. She wanted all of those parts of Mel focused on her.

"Well, I just helped Connie," Georgia heard herself say, trying to steady her breathing. "You're at table twelve. We're—we're at table twelve."

Mel studied her face, her lips turning up in a slight smile. "Perfect. Is there anything I can do?"

"Nope," she said, wondering if the dangerous flush of her makeup-free cheeks was totally visible in the dimly lit banquet hall. "I think we're all done. Oh, actually," she said, "you can get me a drink."

"What'll it be? White wine?"

"Make it a scotch on the rocks," Georgia said, and Mel raised an eyebrow. "I'll have wine with dinner."

"You've got it." She paused, her gaze flickering over Georgia's face. "You look really beautiful tonight."

Before Georgia could respond, Mel turned and made her way toward the bar. Georgia realized she'd been gripping the tape dispenser so hard the plastic casing had cracked. What in the world had come over her? Cool and collected was her thing (with one notable exception, of course, but the Aurelia Martin event was an aberration, not to be mentioned). Now she was falling all over herself just like the throngs of fans who greeted her pop star clients outside stadiums and on red carpets.

Was she teenybopper gaga over Mel Carter? Yes. Yes, she was.

Mel returned with her scotch, and a beer for herself. "Thank you," Georgia said, clinking the bottle Mel held up.

"No, thank you," Mel said, looking around. "I know Connie has been busy taking care of Seamus at home. You're a godsend. Between this, and all the work you've been doing at the shelter—"

"It's been my pleasure," she said. "Connie is my kind of lady."

Mel smiled, just as wide as she'd been smiling the day before after horseback riding, a funny look in her eyes. Like she was happy, or something. Not that Georgia thought Mel wasn't a happy person, it just always seemed like she was the emotional tip of the iceberg. Georgia had no doubt there was a lot going on underneath, but Mel kept a lot hidden. It was nice to see her emote a bit. Let her feelings show.

She linked her arm with Mel's. "Let's go," she said. "I'll show you to our table."

If the boldness of Georgia's touch surprised Mel, she didn't let on.

Georgia led Mel to their table near the stage, gripping her firm bicep through the fabric of her suit jacket. She didn't even need to see a photo of them to know they looked good together. Georgia dropped her shawl and handbag at her spot on the table.

Guests had started to fill in from the front entrance and were assembling near the bar. "Shall we go socialize?" she asked.

"Or just stay here for a minute?" Mel suggested. "Unless you're more interested in schmoozing with members of the town council. Or the head of the PTA from my nephews' school."

"Oh, definitely," Georgia said. "But I can wait. For example, I'm still waiting to hear more about this reputation you have as an amazing dancer."

Mel's eyes sparkled with amusement. "Well, I'm sorry to let you down. But that was just a clever ruse to get you to invite me as your date tonight."

"Ah, I see," Georgia said. "So, what you're saying is I'll have to find a new dance partner?"

Mel gave her a look of mock offense. "What? The pleasure of my company isn't enough? Dancing is overrated."

"So far, so good," Georgia said. "But once the music starts I'll let you know." She took another sip of her scotch and straightened the strap of her dress, causing Mel's eyes to drop to the spot just below her shoulder where she'd adjusted the fabric. Her mind wandered to a fantasy where Mel slid her fingers under that very same strap, tugged it down and to the side, and kissed the bare skin on her shoulders and neck. She shivered with expectation.

"So when you get back to LA, what happens?" Mel said. "Right back to work?"

Georgia nodded. "As soon as I get approval. Just in time for awards season."

Mel nodded, and Georgia thought she detected a flicker of disappointment in her eyes. "So this is the first of a very busy party season for you."

"You got it," Georgia said. She looked around at the room, which was filling up by the second. "Looks like a good one to dip my toes back in. But now I'm spoiled for dates."

"Definitely downhill from here, if I do say so myself," Mel said, her eyes alight with pleasure.

Georgia laughed. It was true. The next party she'd be at, she'd more than likely be alone. Working, but still alone. When was the last time she'd had a date to a party? A date that wasn't Paulina? "Let's go look at the auction items," she said. "I'm not going home empty-handed."

Georgia led the way to the auction tables, which featured gift baskets from local stores, tickets to an upcoming exhibit at the county art museum and even a "book of the month" subscription from the bookstore on Main Street. Guests were bidding on items, and the auction was scheduled to stay open online for one week after the event, allowing people in the town and local cottagers who couldn't attend the evening a chance to bid. "Ooh, I want that!" Georgia said, pointing to a two-night stay at the Briarwood Inn, the elegant lakeside retreat that Hayley had mentioned. The auction tables were crowded, and Georgia took the opportunity to press herself up next to Mel in the crowd.

Mel raised her eyebrows, a playful smile on her face, and placed her hand on the small of Georgia's back. "So, you're planning on coming back to visit after the sale goes through?"

"Maybe," Georgia said, imagining a suite at the inn and waking up with the sparkling waters of Shaughnessy Lake out the window, Mel tangled in the sheets next to her. She hoped Mel didn't notice her blushing. Without breaking away from Mel's touch, she grabbed a pen and added one hundred dollars to the existing highest bid.

"Those are the owners over there," Mel said, pointing to a pretty dark-haired woman holding hands with a man in a gray suit. "That's Grace Bentley and her husband, Noah Crawford. They're talking to Noah's sister, Devyn. My sister thinks Noah looks like Chris Hemsworth."

"I worked with him on a press junket for one of his Marvel films. He has the cutest golden retriever. Goes everywhere with him."

"Is there anyone you haven't met?"

Georgia smiled. "Well, if you must know, I'm dying to meet Patrick Stewart. He's the one famous person I might get tongue-tied in front of."

Mel laughed. "Are you kidding me? What are you, some kind of Trekkie?"

"You don't grow up with scientist parents without escaping with *some* nerdy pastimes," Georgia said. "And come on. He was the ultimate captain. And so debonair."

Mel shook her head. "You're just full of surprises." They were talking so close that if they'd been alone, Georgia would have reached out and grabbed the collar of Mel's shirt to pull her closer. The magnetic energy intensified as Mel locked Georgia in her gaze, and for a moment, she almost felt like they were the only ones in the room. "I'm glad you came here," Mel said quietly. "I wasn't sure about you at first. But I like you."

Georgia lapped up the praise, and felt her breathing become a bit shallower and more ragged. "That feels like a big compliment coming from you," she said.

"Not sure what that means. But okay." Those brown eyes twinkled, and Georgia's stomach did a cartwheel. "So, when you get back to LA, there's really no one waiting there for you? I find that hard to believe."

"Nope," Georgia said. "I don't date. I don't have time."

"Never?"

"Maybe here and there. But let's just say I'm not leaving a toothbrush anywhere."

"Huh," Mel said, her eyes searching Georgia's. "And what would make someone toothbrush-worthy to you?"

Before she could respond, she felt a tap on her shoulder, and turned around to see Connie and another couple in tow. "This is her," Connie said to the man and woman. "Nina's niece."

Before Georgia could react, she was just about bowled over by a thirtysomething red-haired woman with bright eyes and a form-fitting green dress. "Your aunt was the best teacher I've ever had. Period. She turned me from a shy kid with no belief in herself to a confident spelling bee champ after less than three months of being in her class."

"She was my best teacher too," the man chimed in. "She really turned me around in grade eight, when I was going down a bad road. Smoking, stealing my parents' booze, skipping class and spray-painting county buildings late at night. I was going through a tough time with my parents' divorce, and Nina listened to me. 'You are who you hang with,' I remember her always saying! I eventually ditched those friends and got serious about school." His eyes were shining with genuine emotion, and Georgia had to take a deep breath to will away the lump forming in her throat.

"Throw a rock in this place and you'll hit someone who will tell you that Nanny changed their life," the woman said.

"Nina was really special," Georgia said, eyes brimming with hot tears.

"I'm Astrid. This is Grant. We live over on Hollyberry Lake, next to the marina. If there's ever anything you need. Anything at all. We owe her so much."

Georgia could only nod her head and force a smile as the couple said goodbye and left to rejoin the party. She felt a hand squeezing hers and looked up to see Mel's eyes shining with concern.

"You okay?"

Georgia closed her eyes for a moment, the reassurance of Mel's presence helping to calm the waves of emotion washing over her. "I'm good," she lied. The truth was, all she wanted to do in that moment was go back to Nina's, bury her head in the cushions of the corduroy couch and have a good long cry. But Mel's steadfast grip on her hand made it feel right to stay.

"Can I get you another drink?" Mel asked.

Georgia nodded. "Thanks." She returned to their table and sat back in her chair, then watched as Mel wove through the crowd to the bar. Mel said hello and smiled at the other partygoers, politely acknowledging people but not stopping to talk. She still couldn't figure Mel out. There was a warmth and sensitivity there, but for whatever reason, she kept people at arm's length.

What had made Mel decide that Georgia was worth letting in, even just a little bit? She knew Mel was attracted to her. That much was clear. But that invisible barrier that was starting to disappear surely took more than a short-term flirtation to dissolve, didn't it?

She watched Mel weave her way back through the crowd, drinks in hand and eyes locked on Georgia. A wave of something more than mere attraction washed over Georgia. In another world, this might have been the start of something real.

She took a sip of her drink. She would enjoy the night, and not focus on what-ifs.

Appetizers were passed around, and then the guests were invited to sit for dinner. Before she'd even finished her salad, four other Sunset County residents had already stopped by her table to say hello and pay their respects. One of them introduced himself as Jon, which caused Georgia to smile knowingly when he referred to himself as "an old friend."

"You've got her eyes," Jon said, his own eyes watering slightly at the mention of Nina. "I miss her every day." He cleared his throat. "She kept me in line, though, you'd better believe that!"

Georgia had to laugh, but in that moment she wished she'd have tried to convince Nina not to be so practical about her end of life. Why her aunt had put her foot down against having a memorial service of any sort was beyond Georgia. It didn't surprise her at all how many lives she'd touched in the small town, and the people she'd talked to were likely only a small sample size. But then again, Georgia knew exactly why Nina didn't want any fuss—she cared more about other people than herself, and never wanted others to go out of their way for her.

Once Jon left, Georgia tried to turn her attention back to the conversation at her table. Mel was speaking with the man on her right, who was a personal trainer at the local community center. The two other couples across the table were engaged in a debate about which local politician would be the best to take over the mayorship in the next election. Georgia scanned the room, looking at the vibrant community that Nina had been such a big part of, and which clearly felt her loss.

Dessert service wrapped up, and several couples started migrating to the dance floor, where the DJ was playing hits from the '70s and '80s.

"You look like you're in another world," Mel said. "And you need more than cherry cheesecake to cheer you up."

Georgia put down her fork, which she'd been using to push her dessert around on her plate. "Well, if you're offering… I do recall a promise to get out on the dance floor. And if Lionel Richie isn't going to do it for you, I don't know what is."

Mel shook her head and looked at Georgia pointedly. "You know I was kidding. I don't do dance floors."

"I thought you wanted to cheer me up."

Mel opened her mouth to say something, then closed it again. She stood up, then offered her hand to Georgia. "Let's get this over with. Something tells me you're not going to take no for an answer."

Mel led Georgia to the dance floor, which had thankfully become more populated in the last few minutes. This was beyond ridiculous—she did not do dance floors. And yet. Once again, Georgia O'Neill was making her behave in ways that were way outside her comfort zone and made her feel like she was losing control. In more ways than one.

She found a spot in a darker area and turned around to face Georgia as Lionel Richie gave way to "Eternal Flame" by The Bangles. *Of course*. It had to be a slow song.

"Cheesy enough for you?" she asked as Georgia slipped her arms around Mel's shoulders as though it was the most natural thing on earth.

"I love The Bangles," Georgia admitted, coming cheek to cheek with Mel, her words setting off every sense receptor in her body.

"Let me guess. You know them too."

Georgia laughed. "I haven't met The Bangles. But

my best friend, Paulina, and I went to see them at the Troubadour a few years ago. They were amazing."

Mel clasped her hands at the base of Georgia's back, grazing the silky fabric of her dress, and feeling her warm body underneath.

"Thanks for this. And for indulging me," Georgia whispered in her ear. "I'm having a great night."

The warmth of her breath set off a hot tremor deep in Mel's abdomen. "Me too," she said. "You did an amazing job. It looks like people are having a blast." She wasn't looking at anyone else, though. How could she? Georgia's light eclipsed anything near her. Mel circled the pad of her thumb just above where the silky material ended on Georgia's back, where her soft skin was exposed.

"It was fun," Georgia said. "I really like your aunt."

The fact that Georgia got along with her family only warmed Mel's heart further. "Well, she seems to love you. Seamus too." She'd almost forgotten she was on the dance floor at the shelter fundraiser.

"Where are your parents?" Georgia asked. Mel bet they'd love her too.

"They spend the winters in Florida. My sister lives close by, though. She was supposed to come tonight but one of my nephews has the flu. We're all pretty close."

"Lucky you," she said. She smiled, but it was dimmer than usual.

"What does that mean?" Mel asked. The Bangles

crossfaded to Berlin, and it seemed wrong to lead Georgia off the dance floor while she was sharing something so important. And leaving now might mean the night was inching closer to an end.

"Let's just say Nina was more of a parent to me than my own parents. They've always been preoccupied with their research and publishing papers. And up until a few years ago, making sure I achieved as much as them." So Georgia wasn't just a go-getter for her own purposes.

"They're not happy with your career?"

"I don't think they think much of it. There's no PhD attached. They'd like your credentials, though." Mel felt Georgia grip her a little more tightly.

"It's not the be-all and end-all. If you like your job, that's all that matters." The song came to an end, but Mel didn't let go of Georgia's waist. "I would say that was fun, but you might make me do it again," she said.

Georgia's eyes sparkled as Bon Jovi came over the speakers and several other partygoers joined the dance floor, drinks in the air. "You're a great dance partner. Sure I can't convince you to stick around for a few more numbers?"

"Don't push it," Mel said. The truth was, she could have stayed out there all night with Georgia. She no longer cared who knew it—bring on the gossip.

Georgia followed Mel back to their table, and accepted the goblet of water Mel poured her from a pitcher. She took a sip, then stifled a yawn. "Sorry. It's been a busy day. And I didn't sleep much last night."

Mel reached over and tucked a stray hair behind Georgia's ear. "So I'm not boring you?"

"Not in the least. I usually have more stamina. But this town is too relaxed."

"Seems like you needed it. Why don't I drive you home?" She was normally out the door by the time dessert was over, but there was no way she was leaving before making sure Georgia made it home safely.

"No, no," Georgia protested. "The party's just getting underway. And Connie might need help cleaning up."

"That's the event staff's job," Mel said. "You've got some big days ahead."

Georgia looked like she was about to object again, and Mel would have been happy to spend the rest of the night with her—yes, even on the dance floor—but when she yawned again, she nodded. "You're right. I'm exhausted. I'm happy to take a cab, though."

"No way. I'm your date. I'll take you home." Mel stood up and Georgia gathered her purse. They bid farewell to their tablemates, then to Connie, who had finally kicked off her heels again and was on the dance floor with her book club ladies.

Georgia was quiet on the drive home, but at one point, she reached over and put her hand on Mel's, which was resting on the gearshift. If Mel didn't know that the night had been an emotional one for

Georgia, and that she had another challenging few days coming up, she might have considered it an invitation for the night to continue. But, as she pulled up the lane toward Nina's cottage and glanced over to look at Georgia's tired, beautiful face, she was simply grateful to have had an unexpectedly good night.

"Thanks again," Georgia said, unbuckling her seat belt and leaning over to kiss Mel on the cheek. She lingered for a moment before kissing her again softly, this time her velvety lips right on Mel's, warm and perfect and utterly addictive. Mel could have died and gone to heaven.

Mel pulled away from Georgia. "So, this is goodbye, I guess," she said, thinking of Georgia's big plans for her return to LA.

Georgia was quiet as she took Mel's hand again in hers, brushing the fingers of her other hand on top. She looked up at her. "Tuesday night. Come for dinner," she said. "I'm booking a flight for Wednesday. We can celebrate the sale, hopefully, and I can thank you for taking me on at the shelter. Even though I know I wasn't your first choice."

Mel couldn't help but laugh. "Well, I wasn't sure about you at first. That's the truth. But," she continued, "I was wrong. You've been amazing. And I'd love to come over on Tuesday." Why she was prolonging the pain of saying goodbye to Georgia was beyond her, but she'd lost any capacity for sensible decision-making.

"Can I ask you something?"

"No, I'm not doing karaoke with you."

"Ha," Georgia said, "but that wasn't my question. What would make someone toothbrush-worthy to you?"

Mel considered. "I asked you first. We got interrupted before you answered me."

"I'll tell you after you tell me." Her eyes were tired but playful and once again, Mel had no defense.

"To be honest, loyalty is really big for me."

Georgia was quiet.

"And nice boobs."

Georgia laughed. "Hayley said you've basically got women throwing themselves at you. Why aren't you with anyone?"

For a moment, Mel was tempted to make another joke and deflect the question. "I was engaged," she said suddenly. "Her name was Breanne." She was shocked at how easily the words came out of her mouth.

"Was?"

Mel cleared her throat. She couldn't believe she was spilling this to Georgia. "She died. Almost three years ago. Car accident." It still hurt to say out loud, but at the same time, felt like a giant weight off her shoulders.

"Oh, my gosh. I'm so sorry."

Mel was quiet for a few seconds. "It's—it's been hard," she said. "To get over that."

"I can only imagine," Georgia said. "I can't believe

it." The air was still in the car, the talk radio station barely audible in the background. There was no more personal of a conversation than this, but for the first time in a long time, the last thing Mel wanted to do was flee. But she didn't want to dwell on Breanne, and there was no need to solicit any more sympathy from Georgia by sharing anything about Breanne's infidelity.

"And you?" Mel asked, even though the idea of Georgia with anyone else made her clench her jaw. She turned to find Georgia gazing at her intently. "What makes someone toothbrush-worthy?"

"I like aloof brunette veterinarians who play amateur hockey," she said without missing a beat.

It took everything in Mel not to break into a huge smile. "That's very specific," she said. "Are there many of those in LA?"

"I had to travel north to find one." She pursed her lips, then reached over and put her hand over Mel's again. "Come inside," she said quietly.

Mel had been open to conversation, but at Georgia's words and the touch of her hand, talking was now very low on her list of priorities. She turned off the ignition. "Are you sure?" The uncertainty that she'd been feeling about Georgia had all but melted away, and in its place was a craving to have Georgia in her arms again, this time alone.

"Come," Georgia said again, and exited the passenger side without waiting for a response. With the moon lighting the gravel parking area, Mel locked the truck, then followed Georgia up the path to Nina's cottage. She almost stumbled into the dimly lit entranceway, the pounding anticipation making her dizzy.

Georgia pressed Mel up against the door the moment it clicked shut. With her heels on, she was almost at eye level with Mel. "Kiss me," she ordered quietly, and wrapped her hands around Mel's waist. What an hour earlier had been tired eyes were now swimming with lust and intent.

"Bossy," whispered Mel, but the command strengthened her resolve to give Georgia any single thing her heart, or any other part of her, desired. Deeply and hungrily, she kissed Georgia, sweeping her thick tresses back behind her shoulders, then pulling away from Georgia's full lips and sweet breath to trail the tip of her tongue along the nape of Georgia's neck, eliciting a gasp from her open mouth.

"Yes," breathed Georgia.

Mel moved the skinny strap of the dress to the side, and Georgia wriggled slightly, allowing it to fall from her shoulder and inviting Mel to continue trailing kisses along her exposed collarbone. "Bedroom," Georgia said, pulling her by the hand, and Mel was about to say something about all the instructions when they reached the bedroom to find the bed, and every single square inch of floor space around it, covered with clothing, shoes, hair products and makeup.

Georgia's lips turned up in a sexy and mischievous grin. "Sorry," she said, then before Mel knew it, Georgia was tugging her toward the couch.

Mel lay down, still holding Georgia's hand, and pulled her on top so that Georgia was straddling her. Time for her to call some shots. Instinctively, she pulled Georgia against her then started to pull up her dress.

She loved feeling the silky fabric of Georgia's dress, but loved it even more when Georgia allowed her to help pull it over her head in one quick motion and deposit it on the floor. Taking a shallow breath, Mel gazed at Georgia's stunning body, her breasts threatening to spill over the cups of her light pink strapless bra, her still-tanned skin almost sparkling in the moonlight that was beaming through the picture window.

Unable to tear her eyes away from the stunning woman on top of her, Mel started to undo the top few buttons of her shirt, until Georgia brushed aside her hands and took over again. Mel was okay with it. Georgia's hand was trembling as Mel watched her fiddle with the buttons, so she grabbed her hand to steady her. "You don't think this is a mistake?" she asked quietly.

"Nothing about this feels wrong," Georgia said, all breathy but certain, causing a rush of molten lava to

cascade through Mel's veins and pool in the space between her legs. It was all the permission Mel needed
to shed her unbuttoned shirt and pull Georgia's soft,
warm body against hers again, kissing her and ex-
ploring every inch of her exposed skin.

Despite the absolute perfection of what was happening, when Georgia whispered through shallow
breaths that she should close the curtains and stood
up to give them some privacy, Mel steadied herself
for a moment in the darkness of the living room.
Could she, after three years of self-protection and
self-preservation dominating every thought, every
action, every decision, give herself over to Georgia,
in the ultimate act of vulnerability?

As Georgia returned to the couch, she had a split
second to decide, and she went with her deepest,
most uncomplicated instincts. At least three times,
over the course of the following hours—on the
couch, on the floor and back up on the couch once
again, in a tangle of raw passion, submitting to what
they'd both been wanting so desperately. Mel was
thankful it was coming on winter and the closed windows to Nina's cottage kept all of Robescarres Lake
from knowing what was going on inside.

Mel lost herself in Georgia's orbit, Georgia's
tongue, her fingers, her whispers and vibrant energy bringing Mel back to life in an explosion of bliss
that obliterated the emotional and physical purgatory
she'd locked herself in.

She felt so many things: satisfied. Sparkling. Alive.

And in the sweaty afterglow, when Georgia moved up on the couch and laid her head on Mel's bare chest, and she stroked Georgia's hair, watching her body rise and fall along with Mel's breath, she found herself on a cloud of happiness that was higher up than she'd been in a very, very long time.

Hours later, when Mel was awoken by the early call of loons on the lake, she rolled over to find Georgia beside her on the floor beside the couch. Both of their heads were propped up by pillows, bodies covered by the thick blankets Georgia had recovered from a donation pile.

They'd discovered that no matter how tired they were, the couch was comfortable for pretty much anything other than sleeping, but they'd been too tired to relocate and clear the mess in the bedroom.

The morning light seeped through the curtains as Mel slid her hand under the blanket to find Georgia's narrow hip, then moved over to get close enough to kiss Georgia lightly on the shoulder. Her skin was warm and soft, and the sound of her gentle breathing told Mel she was still asleep. Mel trailed her fingertips up and down Georgia's arm, basking in the perfection of her extraordinary figure.

Then, a sharp pang of sadness made her wince. While Georgia was right there beside her, all too real in the moment, it was almost as though she was a mirage, a daydream flash of something that would never be again. It wouldn't be long before she'd be boarding a flight back to her home, to her busy and exciting life, and the night that they'd just shared would be a distant memory.

Georgia murmured softly and turned toward Mel, her hair askew and sleep lines on her cheek from the pillowcase, neither of which prevented her from looking as gorgeous as ever.

"Hey," Mel whispered. "I'd better go." Even though she was resigned to the fact that this was a one-off, staying under the covers with Georgia was still incredibly tempting.

"What?" Georgia asked, propping herself up on her elbow and looking at the clock on the wall. "Not yet. It's so early."

"I don't want to leave. But I have to let Franny out." She slid out from under the blanket, then pulled it back up over Georgia. "You go back to sleep."

"No," Georgia protested, her eyes traveling up and down Mel's bare torso. "I'll walk you out."

Mel gathered her things and watched out of the corner of her eye as Georgia walked naked to the bathroom to get her robe. It had been mostly dark the night before and seeing Georgia now with the faint glint of early-morning sun on her body was something she knew would be forever burned into her brain.

When she joined Mel at the front door, she was wrapped in her robe.

"Thank you," said Mel, after she'd put her shoes on and pulled her keys out of her pocket. "Last night was amazing." It was true. And it was a gut punch that their first night together might also be their last.

Standing on the tips of her toes, Georgia closed her eyes and kissed Mel. "Thank *you. You're* amazing."

It felt so right. For the first time in a long time, Mel wasn't on her way out the door because she was afraid.

In fact, all she could think about was coming back.

"And you were right," Georgia called, as Mel made her way to her truck. "You're a great dancer."

Even though she was heavyhearted, Mel couldn't help but laugh as she slid into the driver's seat and closed the door. She waved at Georgia, who was leaning in the doorway wrapped in her robe, then made the three-point turn back toward the road.

She heaved a giant sigh and focused on driving. It was painful to leave Georgia.

But maybe dance floors weren't so bad after all.

Chapter Fourteen

After a quick shower and a walk with Franny, Mel drove into town to meet Andie for their regular Sunday breakfast while the boys were at skating lessons. Her mind kept drifting to Georgia, flashes of last night and the inevitable sale that likely would be made the next day. Several times she reached for her phone, wanting to check in, tell her she missed her and how much she hoped things would go smoothly. But it also pained her, knowing that the sale meant the final ticks in the clock of Georgia's time in Sunset County. Just as a spark of something that Mel was starting to trust was igniting.

Maybe it's for the best, she told herself as she again resisted the temptation to text Georgia. But for the first time, she was having a hard time believing it.

She entered Swan's Dive, the diner on the outskirts of town, and within ten seconds, a mug of hot water with lemon was in front of her.

"Thanks, Walton," she said to their usual waiter. "How are the lizards?"

"The kids love them. But guess who's cleaning their tank?"

Mel smiled. "You wouldn't be the first. I told you. Make the kids clean an empty tank, or walk an un-tethered leash for a month and you'll see if they'll follow through." She waved off the menus Walton offered, knowing that she and Andie would order the same things as always. Red pepper and mush-room omelet with home fries for Mel, and a green smoothie with a side of bacon for Andie.

She checked her phone to see if Georgia had mes-saged, but found only a text from Connie with a rough estimate of the bids they'd received last night, which in any other year would have been a great news story. And the bids were still open until the end of the week, so that number would only go up. If only the funds were going to something better than covering the costs of closing.

Moments later, Andie came through the door and slid into the booth seat across from Mel. "I saw Uncle Seamus this morning," Andie said. "He doesn't look good."

"He's going to have to retire soon," Mel said. "It's good timing."

"Is the shelter seriously closing? I thought for sure there would be more pushback from locals, or that maybe the county could find some money in the budget."

"Seems like it's a done deal. And I don't know if I can keep up this pace anyway, managing both places."

Walton delivered Andie's smoothie, and she immediately took a big sip. "Knox told me that your new volunteer is really nice."

"Mmm-hmm."

"I also heard she's really pretty." Andie looked at her pointedly.

"She's also leaving town this week. Nina's place is selling tomorrow, probably."

"Too bad," Andie said. "Your complexion's never looked better. I read that falling in love is great for your skin. All that oxytocin."

Mel picked up a sugar packet from the silver caddy on the table and threw it at her sister. "You're ridiculous," she said. "How many times do I have to tell you? You need to stop reading those stupid magazines."

"And you need to stop being such a crusty hermit."

"Whatever. How are the boys?"

"Stop changing the subject."

"Stop meddling."

Andie grinned. "Not until my boys have another aunt. I could use another babysitter."

"You're too much," Mel said, a picture flashing

in her mind of Georgia meeting the boys, them all going out to a movie together, or maybe a day trip to the city for a Blue Jays game. The boys would fall in love with Georgia immediately. Not that Mel would blame them.

She shook her head. No amount of daydreaming was going to keep Georgia from leaving Sunset County.

Mel would see her one last time. Thank her for all her work. And wish her well.

And after that? She was going to be a wreck.

On Monday afternoon, Georgia sat across the desk from Hayley in her real estate office, fiddling with her cell phone, a sick feeling in her stomach. Hayley was sorting through the offers and making notes. There was one hour left until they closed on offers, and from the way Hayley was humming with a smile on her face, Georgia was certain that they'd make the sale that day.

One of the other agents popped her head around the door. "Good luck today, sweetheart," the woman said. "I'm Vibika Tatum. Your aunt and I were in the same book club together. She had a great way of making sure we talked about anything other than the book. But I always learned something from her. You should get a good price today. She always kept that place up so well."

"Thanks," Georgia said weakly, trying to smile.

Vibika left, and Hayley opened the small bar fridge

behind her desk. "Drink?" she offered, looking at her watch. "It's just about happy hour."

"I'm okay," Georgia said. She wanted to be clear-headed when Hayley presented the offers. "I'm going to go for a quick walk, if you don't mind."

"Sure thing," Hayley said. "I'll have everything ready when you get back."

Georgia exited the real estate office into the fiery orange glow of a late-fall day. The sun was starting to descend and reflected a flashlight-beam trail of light off the rippling water of the lake. She walked down the sloping hill of Main Street toward the water, observing the day-to-day life of Sunset County and its residents. The leaves had mostly fallen from the trees, and she knew that soon there would be a thick blanket of snow on the ground. It really was a pretty little place.

She approached a small waterfront area at the end of the street, where a sailboat was coming in to dock and two little girls were skipping rocks on the sandy beach with someone Georgia assumed to be their grandfather.

For what felt like the two hundredth time that day, she pulled her phone out of her pocket to message Mel and cancel Tuesday's dinner, but for the two hundredth time, she changed her mind. She didn't know what to do. Saturday night had been amazing. Beyond amazing. Was it terrible that she wanted to keep it that way? A perfect memory to leave on? Without all the messy complications of saying goodbye. Just thinking about Mel's strong, lean body on the couch underneath her, the fire in her eyes and in her touch—it took her breath away. How was she going to say goodbye, knowing what they could have been?

Maybe canceling was the right thing. She could say she got an earlier flight. She knew it wasn't honest, but was it necessary? Sunset County was really playing with her heartstrings, and besides the serene setting, the open and warm residents and the spirit of her aunt that seemed to exist around every corner, Georgia knew an overwhelming part of the place's hold on her was Mel Carter.

As she slid the phone back in her pocket, it began to vibrate. *Mel?*

But it was Mario Kimpton's name on the screen. Georgia's heart thudded in her chest, and for a moment she considered letting it go to voicemail. How much could she really take in one day? If she lost her job and Nina's place all at once, she didn't know what she would do. She took a deep breath and straightened her shoulders. Better to rip off the bandage.

"Hello?"

"Georgia, it's Mario," he said. "Listen, I know we talked about a slow reentry back to work. And I still think that's important. But we got a call from Jamie Burton's people. His new tour is coming up, and he requested you specifically. I told his team you might not be available, but they're insisting. Any chance you'd consider coming back to meet with them? We'll give you an associate to lighten the load on this one. But it's you they really want. Given what happened, moving you out of crisis management for a bit might be the right move."

Georgia could hardly believe what she was hearing. Not only did she still have a job, but she was being sought after by one of the most exciting rising stars on the planet? It almost made up for being taken out of her new role. But she'd get back there. "I'll be back this week," she said, without missing a beat. "And I'm ready."

After discussing the details of her return, starting with a reintegration meeting that Thursday morning, she said goodbye to Mario and stood for a moment, looking out at the sparkling water in front of her. Sunset County had been the perfect place to get her head back together. To heal. To start to say goodbye to Nina. But it was time to go home.

Georgia looked at her watch. The offers would be ready by now.

She returned to Hayley's office, listened to her advice, and within thirty minutes, Nina's home was signed over to a complete stranger.

Chapter Fifteen

So she was having a goodbye dinner with Georgia O'Neill in a matter of hours. Had she mistakenly taken some of the tranquilizer she usually reserved for her patients herself? Because she was behaving like a loopy, lovesick puppy with no judgment.

No. The truth was, she very much wanted to spend Georgia's last night in town with her. And in some ways, it was the perfect situation. First of all, it was the right thing to do. Georgia had been an incredible help over the past few weeks, and that deserved acknowledgment.

There was no denying that her feelings for Georgia had multiplied unimaginably over the past few weeks, but whether she liked it or not, Georgia was leaving. If anything, this might be the perfect situation. They could have a nice, quiet dinner together, and then there would be closure, and Mel could leave things on a high note, with no opportunity to ever be hurt by Georgia. In some ways, it was the ideal plan.

And then she pictured the look in Georgia's eyes, and the wild abandon with which she'd pleasured every inch of her body. If any of that energy returned, well, it was going to be an interesting evening.

In any event, she had work to do first.

After feeding Franny and taking her for a quick walk, Mel showered, changed and made her way back to the shelter to check on the border collies.

She strode up the path, running through her to-do list in her mind. The dogs, thankfully, were acclimatizing well to their new space. Surely there was comfort in seeing familiar companions, and it was entirely likely that one another's presence was what had kept them alive back in that horrible shack.

Misery loves company, she thought, thinking back to the days after Breanne's death and the revelation of her affair with Lauren, and how when she'd seen Lauren's sunken expression at the funeral, for a single moment, she'd felt less alone. She'd pushed that away quickly, making way for the overwhelming feelings of betrayal and rage that were infinitely easier to give in to.

Lost in her thoughts and the dull exhaustion that coated her like a heavy wool blanket, she almost collided with a red-haired woman in a gray suit, who was turning away from the front entrance. It appeared as though she'd just been knocking— hopefully not loud enough to frighten the shelter's new charges. She wasn't carrying a crate or box or any other type of vessel that people usually used to drop off animals. And technically they weren't open to public visits until noon, so it was unlikely she was there to inquire about an adoption.

"Do you work here?" the woman asked, and it was then that Mel noticed the manila envelope peeking out of her leather briefcase.

"Dr. Mel Carter. How may I help you?"

"Dr. Carter, I have some papers here for Seamus O'Brien. We've been trying to contact the shelter for the last couple of days, but the voicemail has been full."

Full? Had he not checked the messages? Then she remembered the volume of calls they'd been getting since Georgia set up the social media page. Who was this woman, and why had she been trying to get through?

"Callie Davis," she said, sliding the envelope out of her bag.

"What's this?" Mel asked.

"It's the official zoning declaration from the bylaw office. The county has decided to go ahead with re-purposing the building. I'm sure you've—"

"I've heard of the plans," Mel said, through gritted teeth. "I just didn't realize they'd gone through." It took everything in her not to snatch the envelope from her hands and rip it into shreds on the pavement before her.

"If Mr. O'Brien has any questions about the information in the envelope—"

"I'll be sure to tell him to call you, Ms. Davis."

Callie nodded, and Mel stood clutching the envelope, wondering how someone could so coldly deliver the news that they were putting a group of helpless animals out of a home.

Callie turned back just before passing through the gate and shielded her eyes from the sun as she looked at Mel. "I'm sorry this is happening. My family—we got our cat from here. Panda. He died last September but he brought us all the joy in the world."

Mel didn't know what to say, other than the fact that she heard the same story from everyone who'd ever visited them and brought home a new family member of their own. And now it was over.

"Well, goodbye," Callie said.

Mel gave her a quick wave, then let herself into the shelter, breathing in the familiar scent of fur and cleaning supplies that might be off-putting to some, but to her translated to safety.

She tossed the envelope onto the front desk and took a deep breath. "Anything else?" she asked out loud, to no one, to the universe.

There was no time to dwell on anything. She'd have to stop in at Seamus's after this to bring him the letter and the bad news.

As always, working with the animals brought her an inner peace that she was sure rivaled what others got from spiritual practices, maybe doing yoga or guided meditation. The dogs were still hesitant in their new environment, and Mel knew it would take some time before they felt comfortable in her presence. She gave them space, gently petting each one when they allowed, and taking notes on what each one would need when she returned.

How likely was it that they'd find a home for these dogs before the county shut them down?

Mel was sure it wouldn't have been long if Georgia was sticking around. It was a big loss for the shelter, having someone like her to see things that she and Seamus didn't see, to do things they would never in a million years have thought of doing.

Mel sighed. Georgia's departure was a loss in many ways. But, she reminded herself, it was for the best. Because more and more, she knew deep down that Georgia could shatter her all over again, and this time, the damage might be even worse.

Tonight would be a night to focus on saying goodbye. And finding closure.

She looked around at the shelter before locking up. It seemed like she'd have a lot of that to do in the near future.

Georgia rinsed the last mug that hadn't been packed, dried it with a paper towel, then slid it into the small box of Nina's belongings going back with her to California. It was hard to believe that in just over twenty-four hours, she'd be with that box of keepsakes in her pristine apartment, at precisely her favorite time of day, when the LA sunset cast its orange farewell blanket across the city and the city lights started to dot the horizon like fireflies.

She loved being in her place at that hour, on the rare occasions she made it home from work before sunset. She'd kick off her heels and pour a glass of Chablis to take to the balcony to unwind for a few minutes before dinner.

Gazing around the cottage, her 1,200-square-foot home away from home for the past few weeks, she wondered what it would be like to be back in the city. Back to her five-inch heels, artisanal kombuchas and Saturday morning Yoga Sculpt classes at The Body Shop. It seemed like another world away. A world without the tall forest out the windows of the cottage. A world without Anna to make her morning latté and ask her sincerely how she was doing. A world without Taffy, and the bunnies, and the rest of the animals who'd so quickly set up shop in her heart.

A world without Mel Carter.

She glanced at her watch. A few hours until Mel arrived. And then a short time after that, Hayley and Lauren would show up—her parting gift to Mel. Hayley had called Georgia that morning to wish her luck going home, and the idea to invite her to join her and Mel that evening for a celebratory drink had popped into her mind. "Bring your sister," she'd said. "I'd love to meet her." She didn't mention Mel would be there too, so it would be a real surprise for them both.

She was excited to see Mel's reaction, and be part of helping Mel rekindle her friendship with Lauren. They'd all have a great night together, and having Hayley and Lauren there as a buffer would keep Georgia from making any stupid mistakes, like sleeping with Mel again.

Which was all. She. Wanted. To. Do.

But she knew better. And for the first time in her life, the idea of a brief fling terrified her. Because it wasn't just that with Mel. It meant something. It meant too much. And it would make it way too hard to leave.

Mel arrived at seven with a bottle of red wine and a small paper gift bag with silver tissue paper coming out of the top. "Thank you," Georgia said, accepting the bottle of wine. She looked down at the bag. "And what's that?"

"You can open it later," Mel said, shrugging off her jacket, revealing a tight white T-shirt that showed off her lean, athletic upper body. She had dark blue jeans on, and for the first time since Georgia had met her, her hair was tied back in a ponytail, the smooth skin of her neck visible and begging to be touched.

"Come on in," Georgia said. "I have a surprise for you too. But not yet."

Mel raised an eyebrow. "What is it this time? The shelter's on TikTok now too?"

"You'll find out soon," Georgia said. The idea of reuniting Mel with her best friend gave her a shiver of excitement. She knew how much time Mel spent on her own. It would be nice to leave Sunset County knowing that Mel had a friend to call up and spend time with.

She'd put a fire on in the living room and set out a takeout charcuterie box on the counter that she'd picked up from The Peony that afternoon. Gentle flurries were falling outside, some coating the ground like a dusting of icing sugar. "Just paper plates, I'm afraid," she said. "And disposable cups. Everything else is packed up."

"So, this is it. You're really leaving." Mel surveyed the empty cottage, her gaze coming to a stop at the doorway to the bedroom, where Georgia's luggage sat half-packed on the bed, the floor still littered with shoes.

"You sound surprised," Georgia said. "I got my job back." She searched for a reaction from Mel, but she only looked a bit lost as she glanced around the room again. "Have a seat. Let me get you a drink." Mel nodded and sat on the sofa, but she only perched at the edge. Was this going to be an awkward good-bye? Georgia wouldn't let it be. And maybe Mel's old friend arriving would ease the tension a bit, break the ice.

She opened the bottle of wine that Mel had brought, and poured some for each of them. Then she returned to the living room and passed Mel her cup.

"Thanks," Mel said. "Looks like we might be getting some snow tonight."

Georgia sat next to her on the sofa and raised her cup to Mel. "I'm sad I'll be missing the first real snowfall," she said. "Cheers."

"Said no one ever," Mel replied, tapping her plastic cup against Georgia's, then taking a long sip. "So, you've got your job back. Everything is all tidied up. All is forgiven. How are you feeling about going back to work?"

The tone in her voice suddenly made Georgia feel a bit defensive. "I'm feeling good, actually. I'll be starting with a new client when I get back."

"What's it this time? Cheating? Drugs? Bank fraud?" Mel asked, without making eye contact.

Georgia paused. "Actually, the client hasn't done anything wrong. He's a rising star. Squeaky clean. I'm helping him with a press junket for his upcoming tour." She took a sip of her wine, certain that her annoyance was obvious, and felt the need to leave out the fact that the job was almost a demotion for her.

"Squeaky clean, eh? I'm sure that won't last long."

Georgia felt her face heat up. What was this, some kind of guilt trip? "You know, not everyone who's famous is a horrible person. Some of the nicest people I've ever met have been through my work."

Mel's gaze softened. "I'm sorry. It's just—" She put her cup down on the floor beside her and wrung her hands together. "I'm not good at this, Georgia."

"Not good at?"

Mel stood up and moved to the window and looked outside, where the gentle flurries had subsided and a strong breeze was swaying the tree canopy. "I'm not good at goodbyes." She was quiet for a moment, and then she turned to look at Georgia, her expression both fierce and afraid at the same time. "And I really wish you weren't leaving."

I feel the same way, thought Georgia, but she stayed quiet.

"You're the first person I've met in a really long time that I feel a connection with. It's not easy for me. I haven't really shared much with you about my past. I know you think I'm closed off or cold or something. But there's a good reason for that."

Images of Mel tending to the animals, holding her in the back room of the shelter, the light in her eyes when talking about her nephews, took over Georgia's mind. "I don't think that about you. In fact, I think it's the opposite. You're reserved, yes, but that's not all there is to you."

Mel looked outside again, and Georgia stood up and joined her at the window. She placed her hand on Mel's arm, and Mel turned to face her. In no time,

Georgia was in her arms, her head on Mel's shoulder, breathing in the intoxicating scent of whatever laundry soap Mel used. Mel was tall enough that Georgia could feel the softness of Mel's breasts against her collarbone, and as she trailed her hand down Mel's back, the solid firmness of her muscles. She didn't even try to mask the moan that escaped from her mouth.

How was it that a *hug* could be so sensual? They hadn't even taken off their clothes and it was already the second-best sex Georgia had ever had, after Saturday night. She suddenly regretted inviting anyone else over that evening. If a mere hug could light this fire in her and make her quake from the very top of her head, all throughout her body, to the end of every extremity—well, she could only imagine how it would feel to give in again to everything she wanted.

She felt Mel's hand slip under her sweater, her fingers gently grazing the small of her back. "I'll always imagine an ending that didn't have you leaving," she said quietly. Her fingers trailed up Georgia's side, sending a shiver right to her core.

Georgia turned her head slightly and kissed the soft skin of Mel's neck that was exposed by her ponytail. "What's the reason?" she murmured.

"What do you mean?" Mel's fingers continued to trail slowly and gently up Georgia's side, and it was all she could do not to rip off her sweater, and let Mel explore freely all over.

"You said, about your past. There's a reason. You mean your fiancée, right?"

Mel took a deep breath. "That. And I've been really badly hurt before," she said. "By someone I trusted more than anyone in the world."

Georgia pulled back slightly and looked up at Mel, who was gazing down at her. Weeks ago, it would have been impossible to imagine anyone ever hurting Mel. She was so strong. So measured. Impenetrable. But she'd let Georgia in, and now Georgia's mind raced as she remembered the funny look on Hayley's face when she talked about Lauren and Mel's friendship. It suddenly dawned on her that something terrible might have happened there. And that she'd made a huge mistake inviting Lauren.

Just as she opened her mouth to respond, a knock sounded at the front door. Mel looked at her quizzically. "Who's that?"

Georgia's stomach immediately turned to knots. "I wanted to surprise you," Georgia said weakly. The idiocy of her error settled in. It was too late.

Another knock, and then the door swung open.

Hayley entered first, holding a six-pack of beer and a bakery box, and behind her, another dark-haired woman who was almost her twin but with shorter hair and a tattoo showing on the right side of her neck. "We're here!" Hayley called. "Lucky you. You're escaping town right in time for the first dump of snow."

Hayley's smile disappeared and she stopped in her tracks when she saw Mel standing by the window in the living room. Georgia didn't know Lauren but she knew enough to read the expression on her face as one of complete shock.

Mel looked at Georgia, eyes full of hurt and confusion. "Wait." She stopped. "Did you..."

"I thought I'd invite Hayley and Lauren," she said, weakly.

Lauren was giving Hayley the same death stare Mel was shooting at Georgia.

"She didn't tell me anyone else was coming," Hayley said to Lauren. "I'm sorry, I would have told you."

"You three have a great night," Mel muttered, beelining it to the doorway and avoiding any eye contact with her former best friend. "I'm out. Safe travels, Georgia. Good luck with your job."

"Mel, wait," Georgia said, as Mel fumbled with her jacket and her boots at the front door. She was close to throwing up, but she had to fix this. "I just thought—"

"You thought wrong." Mel fixed Georgia in her gaze, her eyes flashing with anger. She grabbed her bag and disappeared out the front door.

Georgia pulled on her shoes and ran outside, where Mel was slamming the door of her pickup truck. The engine roared to life, and the truck's headlights lit up the forest.

She approached the truck, slapping her palm on the passenger's side window. "Mel. Mel! Please!"

She half expected Mel to hit the gas and peel out of the driveway, but the truck idled for a moment, and the window rolled down. "What?" Mel scowled. "I can't believe you'd do that without telling me."

Georgia searched for the right thing to say.

"Actually, I can. You think you're always right, and you're some kind of expert at fixing everything. But you're not."

Georgia choked back tears. "You said you'd grown apart and haven't seen each other for a while. I just thought maybe you'd be happy to see her again."

"You thought that, did you? Based on what?" Mel shook her head, then grabbed the gearshift and put the truck into Drive. She glared at Georgia. "You know, Georgia, you may know *a lot* of people. But the thing is, you don't *know* people at all."

Georgia's eyes filled with tears. "How am I supposed to know you? You're the most guarded person I've ever met."

"Why, because I don't blast every detail of my entire life on social media?"

"It has nothing to do with social media. What are you going to do, push people away forever? Live your life at arm's length?" She gestured toward Nina's cottage. "It's so obvious that you just *bolt* whenever things get hard. Or when you don't want to deal with your feelings." Mel continued to stare straight ahead, a stony expression in her eyes. "The day I ran into you, outside of your house?" Georgia continued. "You couldn't get away fast enough. At the bar? When your teammates recognized me? And that *sock story*, when we were about to have dinner?" Her frustration was boiling over, and she couldn't stop. "Lauren was your best friend. You just looked at her like she was your worst enemy."

Mel's eyes flashed with anger and hurt. "You have no idea."

"What? What was it then? Because all I see is someone who never lets anyone get close. It's pathetic." The second the words escaped her mouth, Georgia was filled with regret.

Mel looked away, and when she turned back to Georgia, her eyes were filled with tears. She took a deep breath. "She *was* my best friend. Until I found out she and Breanne were having an affair," she said, her voice trembling. "They were together the night Breanne died. She got in the car accident because she was rushing to get home from Lauren's place after I arrived home early."

Georgia's stomach lurched. Her instinct was right, and she'd behaved so terribly wrong. "I had no—"

"And for whatever reason, you think I should just go around blabbing that to people. We're different, Georgia. And that's why whatever this thing was between us—" She paused for a moment, her shoulders shaking with a sob. She wiped her eyes on her sleeve. "It was never going to work out." She moved her hand to the gearshift, and Georgia stepped back from the truck.

"What, so you're just going to leave again? Do you ever forgive anyone? Or is it just one mistake and done with you?"

"What does it matter? You're leaving anyway. Goodbye, Georgia."

Georgia took another step back as the window started to roll up and Mel's truck began to move. She watched as it disappeared down the driveway.

She stood alone in the quiet of the evening, numb and unable to believe how quickly the night had gone from being a bittersweet but perfect end to her time in Sunset County, to being a complete disaster.

Georgia didn't have it in her to try to convince Hayley and Lauren to stay, and the two sisters seemed more than eager to get out of there anyway, so an hour later, she sat alone on the couch, cheeks streaked with tears, contemplating making the drive to Toronto and staying at a hotel near the airport rather than waiting until the morning. If there had been an earlier flight, she would have raced to get on standby.

All of a sudden, Sunset County was feeling a lot less warm, and a lot less welcoming.

The gift bag that Mel had brought with her caught Georgia's eye from where it sat on the counter. Georgia retrieved it and brought it with her to the couch, as the last of the light disappeared outside. The sky was velvety and dark, and stars started to dot the deep navy horizon. They were far bigger and brighter here than anything she'd ever seen, like the pegs in her childhood Lite-Brite set, but her own light had dimmed considerably.

She pulled the tissue paper aside and found a small square notecard perched above the gift. Scrawled across the card in Mel's tidy handwriting was a short message. *For next time you're in town*, it read. Tears prickled again in Georgia's eyes as she removed the rest of the tissue paper and pulled out a red collapsible umbrella with a sturdy wooden handle.

A small sob escaped as she remembered meeting Mel out on the road, running back to her place to escape the rain, and Mel offering her clothes and making her tea. The look of concern in her eyes the day she'd arrived at the shelter in tears, after Nina's cottage had gone on the market. How she'd made sure, at every step, that Georgia wasn't overwhelmed the night they rescued the dogs. Georgia buried her head in the couch and let the tears flow. Mel might have had trouble expressing her feelings, but she'd shown her so much care. And Georgia hadn't taken the time to show her the same.

For someone who prided herself on getting things right, on winning, on always being on top of her game, the fact that this was the second major mistake Georgia had made in the span of two months shook her to the core. She'd gotten to a place, thanks to Mel, where she could justify the first one. This one, however, felt like a gut punch. And given Mel's track record, it was unlikely she'd ever be forgiven.

In a few hours, she'd be throwing her things in her rental car and driving to Pearson Airport to make the rest of the journey home. She lay back on the couch and closed her eyes, trying her best to summon Nina's presence and find the comfort of her spirit somewhere in the cottage.

But all she felt was alone.

Chapter Sixteen

On the last night of the auction, a week from the night of the gala, Mel scanned the current highest bids on the online platform. The system was set to close at midnight, in five minutes. The chef demonstration and five-course meal from The Peony was going for a nice four hundred dollars. Someone had bid three-fifty for a custom boat cleaning package from Sudz, and not surprisingly, there had been several hopeful takers for the overnight stay for two at the Briarwood Inn. "Good," she muttered, when she saw that someone had beaten Georgia's bid.

In any other year, it would have been a successful auction, giving the shelter the top-up it needed to stay in operation.

This year, however, it would only cover the costs of shutting down.

Mel scrolled through the list, doing a mental tally of the collected funds. She hit the button to navigate to the second screen of items, then stopped scrolling and leaned forward in her chair.

She squinted at the screen in front of her. Underneath the auction listing for one of the Harris family's kittens was a number with so many zeros after it that it caused her to gasp. The name next to the bid was "Anonymous." There must have been some glitch in the software. Or maybe Mrs. Owen made a mistake on the laptop her grandson had given her last Christmas. Because the amount of the highest bid was more than one hundred times that of the most lucrative auction item they'd ever sold—a pair of courtside Raptors playoff tickets that had been snapped up for a premium price a few years earlier when they won the NBA championship.

This was no small-town silent auction chump change. This was the spoils of a downtown hospital fundraiser.

Mel sat back in her chair, stunned, her mind spinning with what that amount could mean for what up until hours earlier had been a very certain future (or lack thereof) for the shelter.

Who was the bidder? People in the county were certainly generous, and many of the cottagers in the city liked to show their support as well, but this was unprecedented. She had to know if this was for real or a huge mistake.

She clicked on the log-in button so she could see the information in the back end of the system. "Dammit," she muttered, unable to remember the password. Seamus had set it up, so she tried every combination of his and Connie's names, birth years, and the name of their cat, Sassy. No luck. She could call Seamus, but he and Connie were likely fast asleep.

But the computer at the shelter would still be logged in.

Mel grabbed her wallet and keys, Franny sensing excitement and barking behind the door as she locked it and went to her car. "I'll be back soon, sweetie," she called through the door.

Minutes later, she was driving along Main Street, which was lit up by the few streetlights along the small stretch. Everything was closed, except for Pete's Pies, which was in cleanup mode after a busy Friday night of deliveries. As she pulled up in front of the shelter, she was surprised to see the lights on inside. No way Seamus would be there that late. And Georgia's flight had left two days earlier, a fact that made Mel's heart drop every time she thought about it. Mel guessed that it was that very distraction that had made her forget to flick the lights off after leaving that afternoon.

She punched the code on the shelter's front door, but it was already open. Forgetting to shut off the lights was one thing. But there was no chance she would have forgotten to lock up. "What in the hell," she breathed, as she quietly entered the building and listened for signs of an intruder.

At first, all she heard was the low hum of the refrigerator in the adjacent break room, and the whirring of the reception computer's fan. Otherwise, silence.

On the reception desk, the phone blinked, and she walked over to look at it. "You've got to be kidding me," she said aloud again, to no one. The phone screen alerted her to sixty-seven voicemails waiting. Prior to Georgia's arrival, Mel couldn't remember them ever getting more than two in one week.

Something clicked, and she opened her phone and tapped on the Instagram icon that Georgia had urged her to download after Salt and Pepper's adoption. She hadn't been on it since, but when it opened, what she saw confirmed her suspicions about the influx of voicemails.

Every last one of the shelter's animals, both the indoor and the outdoor crew, had its own individual post, with a beautifully shot picture and clever write-up. Even Slinky. Each one also had a series of comments, many indicating that they'd be calling the shelter to inquire about adoption. She shook her head, unable to believe her eyes.

When she looked up, she noticed that the light in one of the examination rooms was on. As soon as she heard the murmur of a voice coming from that room, she knew exactly who was there. And who was the anonymous bidder on the kitten.

Heart pounding, she approached the room, and she took a sharp breath in when she saw Georgia, sitting on the ground, dangling a small knitted ball on a string in front of the orange-and-white kitten, who was batting it around rambunctiously. Her hair was piled on top of her head in a bun, her eyes tired but shining. Georgia looked up at Mel, then looked at her watch. "Bids closed at midnight, right? I came back. I'm bringing him home with me."

Mel swallowed. She couldn't believe Georgia was sitting right there in front of her, thousands of miles away from her home, where she'd only just returned. How many times in the last couple of days had she replayed their last interaction, and how many times had she wished she could take it all back?

She was completely unable to quell the tidal wave of love and desire washing over her. She was still mad at Georgia. But having her back in her presence, a mere three feet away, solidified the fact that she had probably known all along: she was head over heels in love with Georgia O'Neill.

"I know I screwed up," Georgia said, her eyes now misty, and her voice trembling. "I've screwed up a lot lately. But this place—" she stopped, her eyes darting around the room before landing on Mel's "—not just the shelter. But this town…" She covered her mouth, her shoulders shaking with a small sob. "This town," she tried again, slowly, "this town was everything to Nina. And now I understand why."

Mel wiped a tear that was running down her cheek and took a moment to compose herself. "All of that money. Are you really giving that to the shelter? Why?"

Georgia nodded. "It's from the sale of Nina's place. I know you're done with me. But I wanted to do this for Nina. For Seamus. For you. I don't know if it's enough to keep it open. But if not, I can't bear the idea that any of the animals won't find a home. So that should be enough, right? To keep them from getting…" With the sleeve of her sweatshirt, Georgia wiped her tears and runny nose, and it took everything in Mel not to take her in her arms, hold her as close as could be and absolve her of everything she wrongly felt she'd screwed up.

Something shifted inside her. At that moment, Mel knew that she'd forgiven Georgia long before the moment she learned about the donation. She'd forgiven her the very moment she realized that even though Georgia had screwed up, there wasn't a malicious bone in her body, and she was just trying to help. Mel tried to swallow the lump in her throat, but couldn't stop her eyes from pooling with tears. The gorgeous, remarkable woman in front of her hadn't given up on her, even though she'd pushed her away, hard.

"Georgia," she started, her voice gravelly with restraint. "Are you sure? I thought that money was supposed to help smooth things over with your work."

"More sure than I've ever been. This matters more, anyway. And I hope you know how sorry I am."

Mel shook her head, unable to believe what she was hearing. "Georgia, you don't need to apologize. There's no way you could have known. And..." she said, gazing at Georgia's stunning face. "I called Lauren. Yesterday. We're meeting for tea this weekend."

Georgia's eyes widened in surprise as she wiped her cheek. "Oh, wow," she said. "I'm so glad to hear that. What made you change your mind?"

You did. You changed everything, thought Mel. She cleared her throat. "I've held on to it for too long. We may never be friends again. But it's time to move on, or at least hear her out." She took a deep breath. "You taught me that."

The kitten meowed, and Georgia picked him up, holding him against her chest. She smiled through her tears. "I'm calling him Talisman. He's my good luck charm."

Mel took a seat on the ground beside Georgia. She reached over to pet the kitten's downy fur. "He's a lucky guy. Just make sure you—"

Georgia laughed, her amusement bouncing off the walls of the room and filling Mel's heart with warmth. "Get him neutered, I know."

"I was going to say cover your furniture for the first few months. He'll rip it to shreds."

Georgia grinned. "Actually… I might have a new couch coming soon. New to me, at least. It's already a little beat-up." Mel looked confused. "Nina's couch," Georgia clarified.

"I thought that went to Goodwill."

"I called and asked for it back."

"Wait, you're shipping that monstrosity to LA? That's absurd."

Georgia paused. "Not to LA. To Toronto," she said, a glint in her eye.

"What do you mean?" Mel could feel her heart about to leap out of her chest. Was she hearing right?

"It means…it means I've requested a transfer to the Toronto office. Temporarily. It's a bit more low-key there, which is what I need. And I thought—" She stopped, her big eyes looking up at Mel. "I thought maybe I could convince you to forgive me. And that maybe I'd be visiting here every now and then. At last check I also just won the restaurant bid, with one minute left. And I'm going to need a date." She reached out and grabbed Mel's hand. Mel allowed Georgia's fingers to clasp hers, and without thinking, Mel gripped Georgia's hand tightly, as though it would keep her from leaving again.

"On one condition," Mel said, her heart swelling with hope.

"What's that?" Georgia said.

"Stay with me. When you come."

Georgia's eyes shone as she smiled. "Question."

"Yes?"

"Can I leave a toothbrush?"

Mel grinned, love and relief and happiness flooding through her. "I hope you leave a toothbrush."

With that, Georgia was up on her feet, pulling Mel up and then melting into her arms. On the ground, Talisman was meowing again, and within seconds, not only did Mel have Georgia safe in her arms, but Talisman as well.

Talisman. It was the perfect name.

Never in her life had Mel felt any luckier.

Epilogue

"Tilt the left corner a little," Georgia instructed, shielding her eyes against the early March sun with one hand and holding Franny's leash with the other. The late-winter air was freezing, but the sun was helping to keep her fingers from turning into icicles. "No, no, that's too much. There. Perfect."

Mel held the painted wooden sign against the side of the building, just to the right of the front entrance, as the contractor marked the corners so he'd know where to drill the holes to affix it.

"Hold it there so I can see it too," Mel told the contractor, then took a few steps back to join Georgia on the sidewalk. "All good?" Mel said, looking over at Georgia for approval.

The new sign had been delivered the previous

day, and it was made of a richly varnished dark walnut, with gold cursive paint forming the words on it.

Georgia slid her hand around Mel's waist and laid her head on the shoulder of her parka. "She would have loved this." Mel kissed the top of her head, and Georgia felt a peace settle over her that she'd never experienced. Like everything in her life was finally falling into place.

The sign reading Nina Miller Memorial Shelter was being hung beside the shelter's door, the final improvement after a brief closure to make some updates to the animal enclosures and equipment. There was a community party planned later that afternoon to celebrate the reopening.

"Nina may not have wanted a funeral, but she'd have loved this," Georgia said. It was true. The fact that the shelter would now bear her aunt's name made complete sense. She was, after all, someone who changed the lives of so many Sunset County residents. And now she would impact the furry and scaled ones too. Nina would be thrilled to be connected to bringing new life to the town she loved so dearly.

A town where Georgia had been spending a lot more time as of late.

She was enjoying her role at the Toronto office more than she'd expected, and the winter weather wasn't really all that bad if you had the right parka and boots. She remembered an old saying Nina used to recite to her: *There's no such thing as bad weather, only unsuitable clothing.* Once again, Nina was right.

The short drive up north to Sunset County on week-ends, with Talisman—or Tally, as she'd taken to calling him—in his cat carrier on the backseat (with a seat belt on, of course), might have been part of the appeal as well.

"Why don't we go to Rise and Grind, get you your latté, and go for a walk down by the lake? Then we can come back and get set up for the party," Mel said.

"That would be perfect," Georgia said, gripping Mel's hand in hers. She gave Franny's leash a gentle tug, and the dog leaped up.

"I still can't believe we didn't have to close." Mel shook her head. She pulled Georgia closer as they walked arm in arm down Main Street.

"Are you sure this isn't going to be too much for you?" Georgia said. "You've been running on fumes these days."

"No. It feels like the right move. Seamus needs to retire. And he'll be by every now and then. And if I can get a solid associate for the clinic, I can split my time down the middle between there and here."

"Kinda like before, when Seamus hurt his back."

"Kind of. Except without you," Mel said. They were so close together that neither of them even noticed the cool winter breeze coming off the lake.

"I wanted to talk to you about that," Georgia said. "I love my job. And I don't want to give it up. But more and more it seems like a lot of what I do can be done online. I want to be here more. I want to be with you."

Mel brushed a strand of hair from Georgia's face and leaned in to kiss her softly, her lips warm despite the cold. "You saved more than just the shelter, you know," she whispered. "You saved me. I want you here as much as you can be."

"We saved each other," Georgia said. "I love you, Mel."

"I love you too," Mel said softly, and she kissed Georgia again, this time more deeply, more urgently. A passing car honked, and they both started to laugh. "You know, a few months ago no one in this town knew any of my business. And now I feel like you've made me the poster girl for PDA."

"You don't mind," Georgia said, feeling her grin stretch from cheek to cheek.

"Next thing you know I'll be back on some kind of dance floor again."

"Speaking of which, there's an event in the city next week I'd love for you to come to—"

Mel put her face in her hands, and shook her head dramatically. "Only you, Georgia O'Neill. Only you."

Georgia grabbed Mel's hand, raised it in the air and spun her around. "You love it."

Mel's eyes sparkled as she pulled Georgia in close. "You know I do."

* * * * *

Get 3 FREE REWARDS!

We'll send you 2 FREE Books plus a FREE Mystery Gift.

FREE Value Over **$20**

Both the **Harlequin® Special Edition** and **Harlequin® Heartwarming™** series feature compelling novels filled with stories of love and strength where the bonds of friendship, family and community unite.

HARLEQUIN
PLUS

Try the best multimedia
subscription service for romance
readers like you!

Read, Watch and Play.

Experience the easiest way to get
the romance content you crave.

Start your **FREE TRIAL** at
<u>www.harlequinplus.com/freetrial</u>.